SPICY MYSTERY STORIES

August 1935 Issue

SPICY MYSTERY STORIES for August 1935

Published by:

Wildside Press
P.O. Box 301
Holicong, PA 18928-0301 USA
www.wildsidepress.com

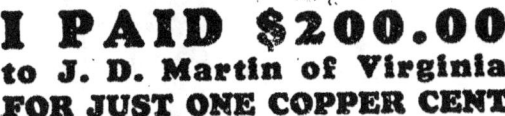

When answering advertisements please mention SPICY MYSTERY STORIES

1

SPICY MYSTERY STORIES

August, 1935   Vol. 1, No. 4

CONTENTS

SPICY MYSTERY STORIES is published by the Culture Publications, Inc., 900 Market St., Wilmington, Del.

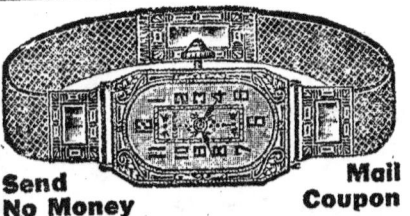
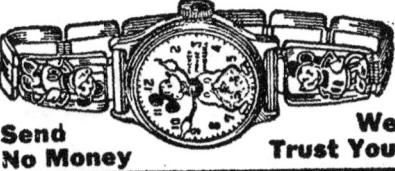
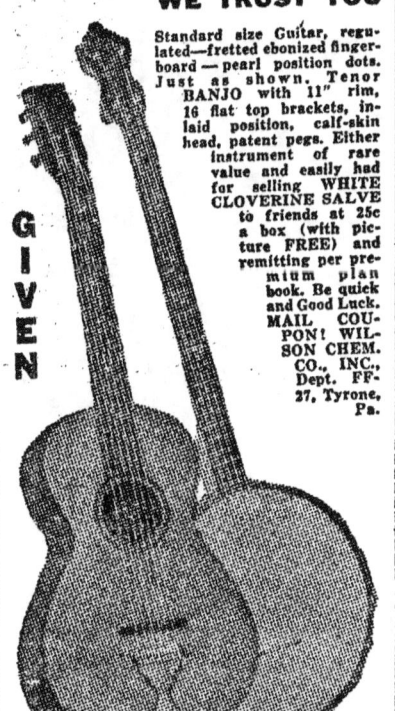

TRY—WILSON'S COUGH DROPS—5c EVERYWHERE

By
ROBERT LESLIE BELLEM

THE

Could the headsman win a woman's heart? Could love escape the shadow of his grisly trade? . . . The weird, powerful story of a passion choked in blood—and two fates twisted beneath the fatal axe

NOW, that was a queer thing, Gerard thought. The nurse had spoken to him in German. And although his memory of the tongue had almost vanished, he understood her perfectly. But why should a nurse in a New York hospital speak German? And the room seemed vaguely strange. Even the bed on which he lay had a different feel.

He remembered the accident that had sent him to the hospital. He had been struck down by a taxi while crossing

wasn't quite sure. Everything seemed a little hazy, a little blurred.

Once more he heard the nurse's soft, soothing voice—in German again. "You are now well, *Herr* Gerhardt. You have recovered from your injuries. We are going to let you go home today."

Bill Gerard frowned. He couldn't quite understand why she insisted on calling him *Herr* Gerhardt. Of course, Gerhardt had been his family name originally, back in Germany. Wilhelm

Columbus Circle. He had been unconscious a long time. He recalled having heard a dim, far-away voice when he had first been taken from the ambulance.

A doctor had said, "Mr. Gerard has a brain concussion. He must be kept very quiet, very still." That had been yesterday—or the day before. Gerard

Gerhardt, he had been christened. But that had been so long ago that he scarcely remembered it. That had been back in Berlin, when he was a small child.

He tried to piece the puzzle together in his mind. When he was only six, his

EXECUTIONER

He swung the axe over the gray-hooded figure of the kneeling girl . . . and something strange—terrible—tore at his heart.

mother had brought him here to New York; had Americanized his name to William Gerard. He hadn't set foot out of Manhattan since that time—and that had been twenty-five years ago. And now, at the age of thirty-one, he was being addressed as *Herr* Gerhardt. It was damned queer.

Of course he still had relatives living back in Berlin who stuck to the Germanic spelling of the name. In fact, he had a twin brother somewhere in Germany.

He hadn't seen this twin brother since their separation in childhood.

Gerard's parents had divorced. The mother had emigrated to New York with one of the twins. The father had remained in Berlin with the other. There had never been any correspondence. The twin brothers had never seen each other again. Bill Gerard had almost forgotten the existence of his German brother.

NOW he frowned. The nurse had called him *Herr* Gerhardt. There was something wrong somewhere; because in spite of his puzzlement, the name seemed as familiar as though he had never borne any other. Gerhardt seemed more natural than Gerard. Why was that?

He looked up at the nurse. She was leaning over him. She was the pure, blonde German type, lovely of features and complexion. She was husky—no denying that. She had hips. Her full breasts were almost matronly in their rounded, fleshy contours.

Still, a girl of her stature could stand such full-blossomed generosity of curves. And anyhow, Gerard liked big girls. Abruptly he knew that he liked this yellow-haired, smiling nurse. Liked her lots.

As she leaned over his bed, the front of her uniform fell away from her white throat. Gerard could see the deep, enticing valley between her firmly-heavy breasts; and the sight stirred a deep surge of emotion in his body. "You are very nice to me, *Fraulein,*" he said. He was startled to hear himself pronounce the words in flawless German. And yet it seemed natural enough.

The girl smiled down at him. She had delicious dimples, and her eyes were like two blue pools in a forest. "Have you forgotten that I gave you permission to call me . . . Kathy?"

"Kathy!" he said. "What a pretty name!" He caught her hand and held i[t] imprisoned between his palms. He coul[d] see the swelling contours of her bosom through the starched white uniform sh[e] wore. He pulled her downward towar[d] him. She giggled as he thrust his finger[s] into the neck of her dress . . . "What No brassiere, Kathy?" he whispered.

"Not since you—you asked me to sto[p] wearing one," she answered.

Gerard stiffened. He didn't remembe[r] anything about that! He didn't remembe[r] ever having seen this particular nurs[e] before. . . But wait! A dim, bewildere[d] recollection was growing in his mind—

"Tell me, Kathy. How long have [I] been here?" he demanded.

"Why—two weeks, *Herr* Gerhard[t.] Don't you remember?"

"And what hospital is this?"

"The *Wilhelmstrasse* Lutheran, o[f] course!" She stared at Bill Gerard, a[s] though puzzled. An odd, suddenly-fear[-]ful light crept into her eyes. Her bod[y] quivered, as though with an inwar[d] shudder. She pulled away. "You—yo[u] seem a little—queer, *Herr* Gerhardt[!]" she whispered. "As though—as thoug[h] you were not yourself!"

"I wonder!" Bill Gerard mutterec[.] Things were becoming increasingly haz[y] to him. For some weird, inexplicable re[a]son, he began to feel that he was not i[n] New York. This was Berlin. Strange—but he was beginning to forget abou[t] New York. He couldn't quite remembe[r] what it looked like. . .

AND the consciousness of Berlin wa[s] growing on him steadily. He trie[d] to speak a few words of English. Th[e] sound was thick and harsh on his tongu[e.] Kathy, the blonde nurse, paled a littl[e]

"You are not well!" she gasped. "You are suffering a relapse! I must call the *Herr Doktor*—"

"Don't. Please don't. I'm quite all right now," Bill Gerard lapsed again into German. "I'm quite myself. I'm Erich Gerhardt, and there's nothing wrong with me."

"*Gott sei dank!*" the nurse whispered. "For a moment I was frightened—" She stared at him. "You even ... even *looked* different! But now you are yourself again. You—you are sure you feel well?"

"Perfect!" he grinned at her. It dawned on him that he must have been dreaming; must have been delirious. What had ever given him the idea that he was Bill Gerard of New York? A ridiculous fantasy of disordered imagination. He knew who he was, now. He was Erich Gerhardt; he was a Nazi official; and he had been run down by a taxi on *Unter den Linden*, two weeks ago. Odd, how for a moment he had imagined himself to be William Gerard of New York!

He yawned. "And you say I am to be released from the hospital today, Kathy?"

"*Ja wohl.* Are you glad, Erich?"

"Not very."

"But why not?" she stared at him.

"I'll miss you," he smiled into her eyes.

She colored. "But—are we not going to be together? Did you not say—"

Suddenly he remembered. "Of course! For the moment I forgot, Kathy. My head is a little thick today. You are going home with me. You are going to nurse me through my convalescence!"

"You—you still want me—?"

He grabbed her and pulled her down upon the bed. "Want you? *Gott!* I cannot wait until we are alone together—where we will not be disturbed. . .!"

He kissed the warm, throbbing hollow of her creamy throat. "When we are alone in my apartment in Brooklyn—" he whispered.

She drew back. "Brooklyn?"

He laughed. "Now, what in heaven's name made me say that? I must be crazy today. I meant my flat in *Konigsplatz*, of course." He rolled over on the bed and made her sit down beside him.

At first she struggled to get up; but when he had unfastened the neck of her starched white uniform and found the soft curves of her breasts with his hands, she submitted with fierce willingness.

She pressed his palms until his fingers sank deep in soft, fragrant woman-flesh. When he kissed her, she parted her red lips so that he could experience the tingling, electrical thrill of her moist, darting tongue. . .

THE door of the room suddenly opened. A man stepped in; stared; stopped dead in his tracks. He was tall, erect with a military stiffness; his hair was close-cropped and his eyes close-set, narrow. "Well!" he rasped.

Kathy leaped from the bed, trying to fasten the front of her mussed white uniform. Bill Gerard scowled. "Who the devil are you?" he barked out. "Who asked you to come in here?"

"*Herr* Gerhardt, I would have a word with you in private," the tall man snapped. Then he turned to the white-faced nurse. "*Fraulein* Kathy—get out!" he spat venomously.

Gerard got out of bed, tried to stay the nurse; but she eluded him and ran from the room. Then Gerard faced the newcomer. "What right have you to—?" he began angrily.

"Mind your tongue, Gerhardt! Do not forget that I am your superior officer!"

Abruptly, Gerard remembered. This

was Graf Von Kemmerer! Queer that he hadn't recognized him until now! And what in the world had possessed him to address his superior so disrespectfully? Gerard flushed. "Your pardon, Count. I—my mind is a little hazy today. Half the time I find myself imagining that I'm an American named Gerard, in New York. I—"

Von Kemmerer's narrow eyes flashed. "It was also a mental aberration, no doubt—your making love to your nurse?" his voice dripped sarcasm.

Something in the man's manner seemed to send a chill into Gerard's blood. Von Kemmerer's lips were thin, cruel; his eyes held little flickers of evil. Within Gerard's brain, an unvoiced sixth sense seemed to be whispering of danger. . . .

There was something sinister and implacably ominous about the man's ferret-like gaze. A crepitant fear tightened Gerard's scalp, made it crawl on his skull.

Von Kemmerer spoke again. "I should think that one in your position would find it difficult to win the love of a woman, *Herr* Gerhardt!" he grinned a vulpine grin.

"In my position?" Gerard was puzzled. "What do you mean?"

The Count shrugged. "Let it pass. You are obviously not yourself. Perhaps I should delay the mission that brings me to you." He half-turned to depart.

Gerard spoke quickly. "Nonsense! I'm quite all right. What is this mission you spoke of, *Excellenz?*"

Von Kemmerer's eyes bored into Gerard's. "It is a command from the *Reichsfuehrer—Herr* Hitler, the Chancellor."

"A command—for me?"

"*Ja.*" Von Kemmerer reached into a pocket of his coat and extracted a sealed manila envelope that bore the red swastika insigne of the Nazi government.

"I have here a certain list of party members who are suspected of disaffection for the cause. There is soon to be a blood-purge. *Der Fuehrer* wishes the list entrusted to your keeping until he is ready for it. Since you are leaving the hospital today, you will take it home with you and guard it well until it is called for."

"But—but why should it be entrusted to me?"

"Your particular—or should I say peculiar—position in the party is unknown to the public at large, *Herr* Gerhardt. Very few are aware of your—er, official status and duties. Hence, it is not likely that spies would suspect you of possessing this list. It should be safe with you."

GERARD accepted the sealed envelope. A hundred questions hammered within his mind. But some inner intuition forbade his voicing them. That he was an official of some sort in the Nazi government he knew; but the nature of that position was hazy and indistinct to him.

It was as though a veil had been dropped over part of his conscious memory, so that he could see but partially. . .

He drew his bare heels together and snapped out a Nazi salute. "*Sehr, gut, Graf Von Kemmerer!*" he said quietly. "I shall guard the list well."

Von Kemmerer grunted as he strode out of the room.

Later that day, in his apartment in *Konigsplatz*, Gerard held the blonde Kathy in his arms. She seemed strangely troubled, and her blue eyes were turbulent pools of vague presentiment.

"That man—that Von Kemmerer—he frightens me!" she whispered.

"Why should you be fearful of him? On what grounds?" Gerard's voice was warm, soothing, comforting.

"He—he means harm to me. I can feel it."

"So!" Gerard stiffened. "That's why he looked like a thunderbolt today at the hospital, when he discovered you in my arms!"

"Ja. And—I—I fear his vengeance. He is a bitter enemy—relentless and hard. When his eyes glared into mine, I felt that . . . something horrible is going to happen. Oh, Erich—hold me! Hold me tightly! Don't let . . . anything happen to me. . .!"

"Never fear. I shan't!" Gerard crushed her feminine body against him

Von Kemmerer leered from the doorway. "Remember, I am your superior officer!" he snapped.

"But why should he wish you harm, Kathy darling?"

"Because he is jealous!" she flung out.

"Jealous?"

She hung her head. "I—I have a confession to make, Erich. You are not . . . the first man in my life. . ."

He laughed in his throat. "What of it? I have never questioned you about your past, have I?"

"But . . . I was once Von Kemmerer's . . . mistress."

with an ardent desire that leaped, like an electric arc, from his questing hands into the yellow-haired girl's veins, binding him to her with vibrant thralls of ecstasy.

He drew her toward a divan, sank with her upon its silken cushions. The flesh of her thighs seemed hot to his seeking, exploring fingers. . . The kisses he stormed at her eyes, her lips, her throat were fiery, laden with longing.

She made no struggle when he unfastened her frock, drew it down over her shoulders to disclose her firm-fleshed breasts. . . Her shirt had twisted up toward her lush hips. . .

LATER, Gerard remembered that sealed envelope; the one which Von Kemmerer had entrusted to his keeping. He had left it in the inner pocket of his discarded coat. Now he retrieved it.

The very feel of the envelope seemed to impart a sinister tingling to his fingers, so that his hand grew a little cold. Kathy, on the divan, watched him as he went toward a desk-drawer.

He opened the drawer, seeking something. He frowned. "That's odd. I had a strong box—!" he muttered. Then his eyes grew narrow. "But that strong-box in in my Brooklyn apartment!" He drew a sharp breath. For an instant, it had seemed as though the veil had lifted from his mind; that he was once more William Gerard of New York. Then the elusive hallucination vanished. "I don't know what ails me today!" he exclaimed. "I have the queerest ideas. . ."

"Ideas?" the blonde Kathy's tone was troubled.

"As though I were two persons instead of one. As though I were living two lives. Almost as though I were not Erich Gerhardt—not here in Berlin!" Even as he spoke, the weird sensation was erased from the tablets of his memory. With the assurance of long practice, he went to a wall-safe at the far end of the room, twirled its combination dial, opened it and thrust the sealed envelope into the steel-lined aperture. He closed and locked the safe.

"What was that? What was it you put in the safe, Erich?" Kathy's eyes were curious.

"A State document. Von Kemmerer gave it to me for safe-keeping."

"Are you—are you connected with the Nazi government, Erich?" Kathy asked sharply.

Gerard smiled. "Yes." He was glad she did not ask him what his official capacity might be. Because he didn't know. It was one of the things he couldn't remember. . .

It was late that night when he experienced his next sensation of inexplicable double identity. He had been sleeping. Kathy lay by his side, her breasts moving gently with her even breathing.

Her body was warm and fragrant, and in the faint light of a street-lamp that filtered through the bedroom window, Gerard could see a tiny, tired, little-girl smile at the corners of her kiss-swollen mouth. And then he heard a sound.

It was so soft that it just barely reached his ears. Soft, slithery, creeping . . . as though someone—or *something*—might be moving about in the next room.

Gerard sprang lightly from the bed. He started toward the adjoining living-room. He brought up sharply against the bed-chamber's blank, solid wall. He experienced the feeling common to many who are awakened suddenly. He couldn't orient himself; couldn't remember the direction of the door he sought.

And yet this was different. The door should be right here. "But that's in the Brooklyn flat!" he whispered to himself; and immediately wondered what had made him say it. He'd never been in Brooklyn. Had never been beyond the borders of Germany!

Abruptly, the blackness of the night seemed to close in upon him like a stifling shroud, throttling his brain until it was impossible to think clearly. . .

IT WAS a full minute before he realized where he was; before he recognized his surroundings. Then, in the darkness, he found the door and went into the living-room. He snapped on the lights. There was nobody there. Nothing was disturbed.

He returned to the bed. Kathy opened her blue eyes, sleepily. "What is it, sweet?" she whispered.

"Nothing. A bad dream." He held her in his arms, as though fearful that she might vanish before his eyes. A strange dread took possession of him. He had the feeling that Kathy was unreal, that everything was unreal. Yet her body was warm in his arms; her breasts tender and throbbing to his touch.

She shivered against him. "I have a terrible feeling of evil!" she whispered tremulously. "As though . . . as though you were about to . . . kill me . . ."

"Gott!" he rasped. "Don't say such things, Kathy!" But goose-flesh crept over his skin like squirming maggots; because—*he had just experienced the same thought—!*

They lay awake until dawn, silent, afraid. . .

In the morning, Kathy went to the store for breakfast eggs. And while she was gone, Gerard heard an imperative knock on the front door of his apartment.

He answered the summons, opened the door. Graf Von Kemmerer stepped into the room. The man's ferret eyes bored holes in Gerard. *"Guten morgen, Herr Gerhardt!"* he snapped out. "I have come for that envelope. *Der Fuehrer* wants it back."

"Very well. I'll get it for you," Gerard answered in the German that had become second nature to his tongue. He turned, went to the wall-safe, opened it.

His eyes widened; and a sudden cold sweat stood out on his forehead, trickled down his ribs from his armpits. His hand delved into the steel-lined recess in the wall, fumbling, questing frantically.

"Is something wrong, Gerhardt?" Von Kemmerer rasped.

"The envelope—is—gone!"

"You jest!"

"*Nein!* It is not here. I placed it in this safe, yesterday. Now it is not here. I—"

"You have betrayed your trust, Gerhardt! It is my duty to place you under arrest at once. You will put on your coat and hat and come with me."

"But—"

"Schnell!" Von Kemmerer snarled gutturally.

Gerard's shoulders sagged, and a vast, ominous weight seemed to be pressing his heart, squeezing it dry of blood. . . He felt a weird sense of impending disaster, as though the wheels of some demoniac fate was turning, drawing him inexorably toward a black, slavering maw of hell. "I—I should like to leave a little note here—" he whispered.

"For the woman who is your mistress? There will be no time for that, Gerhardt. You will come with me. Right now!"

Gerard got his hat, his coat. He shambled apathetically after Von Kemmerer; and as he left the apartment, closing the door after him, it seemed that he was ending an episode.

LATER, confined in an antechamber off Von Kemmerer's office in the *Wilhelmstrasse*, his mind grew more and more lethargic; refused to function except in spasmodic flashes. And then, after long hours, Von Kemmerer himself entered the antechamber. He was smiling a thin-lipped, wolfish smile. *"Herr* Gerhardt, you are released. The envelope has been recovered. And now the Chancellor himself wishes to see you."

Some force—something beyond himself—urged him toward the girl. What had happened to him? Was he somebody else?

Gerard's eyes widened. "I am free? *Der Fuehrer* wants me?"

"*Ja.* Do not keep him waiting."

Gerard went out into a long, marble corridor. He climbed a flight of white, broad stairs. He approached a door.

A sentry barred his path. "I am Erich Gerhardt. *Herr* Hitler has sent for me," Gerard spoke quietly.

"*Gut.* He is waiting for you. Go in." Gerard noticed that the sentry seemed to shiver and draw aside as he passed the man; as though the fellow were unwilling for Gerhard to touch him as he went by.

Faintly puzzled, Gerard stepped into an elaborate room. Behind an ornate desk sat a man, round-faced, commanding. A stray lock of hair hung down over *Der Fuehrer's* forehead; his moustache twisted as he smiled a greeting. "Good morning, Gerhardt. You have been notified that there is work for you this afternoon?"

"Work? This afternoon? *Nein.*" Gerard felt a growing bewilderment. If only he could remember what his duties were in the Nazi organization!

The Chancellor frowned. "Von Kemmerer should have told you. There is a spy to be executed. You will prepare yourself in the usual manner. Full evening dress, top hat, white gloves. The axe will be well sharpened, I promise you."

Like a blinding flash of lightning bursting within his brain, Gerard suddenly knew. *He knew!* He was—

12

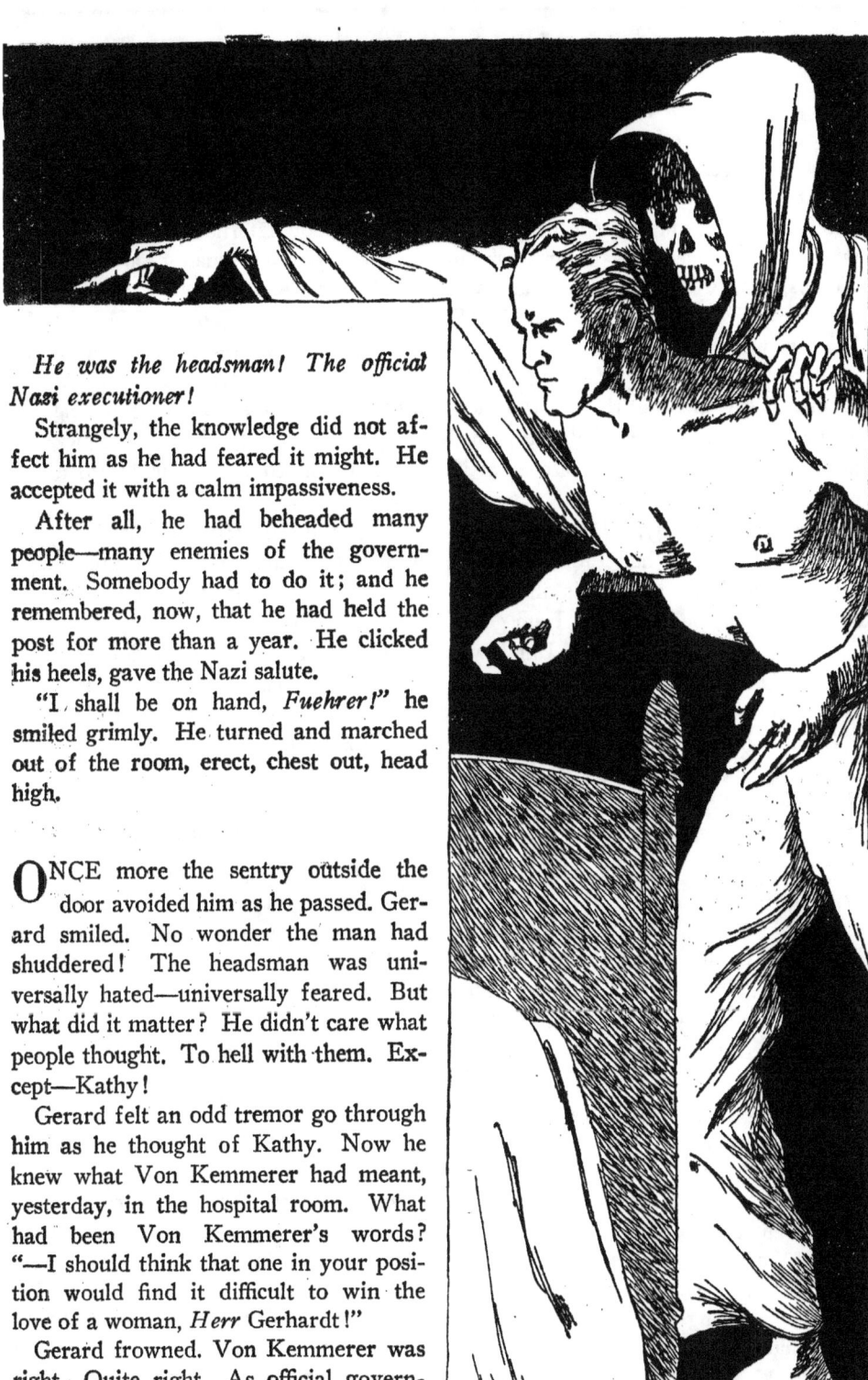

He was the headsman! The official Nazi executioner!

Strangely, the knowledge did not affect him as he had feared it might. He accepted it with a calm impassiveness.

After all, he had beheaded many people—many enemies of the government. Somebody had to do it; and he remembered, now, that he had held the post for more than a year. He clicked his heels, gave the Nazi salute.

"I shall be on hand, *Fuehrer!*" he smiled grimly. He turned and marched out of the room, erect, chest out, head high.

ONCE more the sentry outside the door avoided him as he passed. Gerard smiled. No wonder the man had shuddered! The headsman was universally hated—universally feared. But what did it matter? He didn't care what people thought. To hell with them. Except—Kathy!

Gerard felt an odd tremor go through him as he thought of Kathy. Now he knew what Von Kemmerer had meant, yesterday, in the hospital room. What had been Von Kemmerer's words? "—I should think that one in your position would find it difficult to win the love of a woman, *Herr* Gerhardt!"

Gerard frowned. Von Kemmerer was right. Quite right. As official government executioner, he was a pariah—an outcast. If Kathy ever found out his real status in the Nazi party, she would turn from him with loathing—

"She must not find it out!" Gerard whispered harshly to himself. "I love her. I cannot lose her. She must never know! I'll keep it from her, some way!"

But he was still uneasy, still vaguely fearful that she might suspect the truth, when he entered his apartment in *Konigsplatz*. As he opened the front door he called out. "Kathy! Darling!"

There was no response.

Gerard went swiftly through all the rooms. Kathy was not there. And then, in the bedroom, he saw the note pinned to his mussed pillow. He snatched at it, read it.

It was from Kathy. "Darling Erich," it read, "I have just had a message from the hospital. My mother is ill at her home just outside Potsdam. I am going to her, stay for a day or so. But I will return. Until I see you again, a million kisses from—Your Kathy."

Gerard smiled. He felt an inner satisfaction that Kathy was temporarily gone. Now she would be out of the city when he fulfilled his gruesome duty that afternoon. There would be no cause for her to suspect. . .

WHISTLING blithely, carelessly, he bathed and donned his impeccable evening clothes—starched white shirt, satin-striped trousers, white tie, tail coat, snowy gloves. His opera-hat he flattened and thrust into a bag. He slipped into a light top-coat that concealed his costume; drew a cap over his head, down over his eyes. He went out.

He went around the apartment-house toward the rear, where his roadster was garaged. Then he stopped short. What in hell was wrong with him? He had no car! That was . . . in Brooklyn? "Bah!" he snorted. "Nightmares again!" He strode off, whistling.

They were ready for him at the place of execution. Von Kemmerer was standing by the headsman's block, flicking at the brownish stains of dried blood with his military stick. Von Kemmerer was smiling. "You are on time, *Herr* Gerhardt. Good afternoon." His voice had a silky, purring quality, and his eyes were narrowed, cat-like.

Gerard nodded shortly. He discarded his cap and his top-coat. He popped out his opera-hat, settled it firmly on his head. There was a huge, glittering axe standing against the block. He picked it up, tested its edge. The blade was razor-sharp, murder-honed.

"Your mask, *Herr* Gerhardt." Von Kemmerer extended a silken domino.

Gerhard took it, slipped it over his eyes. "Thank you."

Von Kemmerer's pointed teeth were bared in a sadistic, anticipatory grin. "Do you know whom you are beheading this afternoon, *Herr* Gerhardt?"

"*Nein.* Who is it?"

"The person who stole that envelope from your safe last night. Your stroke will not only avenge the State, but it will cleanse your own honor as well."

Gerard grunted. "Let's get it over with. I think I shall go to Potsdam when I have finished."

Von Kemmerer grinned. "*Ja?* Very well." He raised his voice, issued a sharp command.

A door opened slowly in the great, grey-stone building beyond. Into the courtyard filed a solemn procession of guards, jailers, a chanting priest. Gerard stared. In the center of the group, held upright by two sentries, was a woman!

She was clad in grey prison uniform, and the black hood of the condemned prisoner was drawn loosely over her head, completely concealing her face.

Gerard scowled. "A woman? Why didn't you tell me? Women make trouble. Their long hair dulls my axe!"

"But you will strike true, *Herr* Gerhardt. You will strike true, to purge your own honor." Von Kemmerer's voice was a sinister whisper.

Gerard frowned.

AND then they had forced the grey-clad, hooded woman to her knees in front of the block. Had shoved her head downward until it rested upon the blood-stained wood. Through the hood, Gerard heard her strangled voice. "I am innocent. . .!"

Gerard grunted. They were all innocent, to hear them tell it. He hefted his axe, raised it high over his shoulders. He took aim. . .

The blade flashed momentarily in the sun. Abruptly, Gerard stiffened. What was he doing here? What was he, Bill Gerard of New York, doing here with a headsman's axe? It was fantastic. . .

The feeling vanished as swiftly as it had come. He was Erich Gerhardt, Nazi executioner. He brought the axe downward in a singing, swishing arc.

There was a cry; the chunking sound of sharp metal cleaving through living flesh and shuddering bone. The axe was stuck in the hard wood of the block, inches deep. Twin streams of crimson spurted horribly, like red jets from a fountain. . .

Something round rolled at Gerard's feet, came to rest by his toes. He looked down, almost disinterestedly.

"God! *God in Heaven!*" he cried out.

The hood had fallen away from that severed head. Blue eyes stared up at Gerard; red lips moved, as though seeking to say something. . . *It was the head of Kathy!* And the lips were still moving, twisting, grimacing horribly. . .

Gerard heard the clicking sound of Kathy's white teeth gnashing together. . . Her yellow hair was wet and clotted with blood. . .

Von Kemmerer laughed harshly. "So!" he snarled. "You have killed her. Because I willed that you should. Because I stole that envelope from your safe last night, and later planted it in her clothes!" he gestured toward Kathy's headless body.

"I forced her to write that note and pin it to your pillow before I took her from your apartment. That was while you were confined in my office; it was to keep you from suspecting the identity of your victim!" He laughed again, wildly, insanely. "She left me. She preferred you. Well—you're welcome to her now!"

Gerard stared. His breath choked in his throat. Kathy—his Kathy—he had killed her!

MADNESS descended upon his turbulent, seething brain. "You swine!" he cried out savagely. He raised the bloody axe, sprang at Von Kemmerer. The man stepped backward; tripped over Kathy's severed head, slipped in her viscous blood—

Gerard brought down the axe. Its blade split Von Kemmerer's skull from crown to chin, and Von Kemmerer's brains spewed out to mingle with the crimson gouts from Kathy's severed arteries. . .

Gerard turned, raced for the open door through which they had brought Kathy. As though frozen, the guards and the sentries made no move to stay him. He leaped into the building, sped up flight after flight of stairs. He was on the building's roof.

Pursuing footsteps were pounding after him now. He lurched toward the

(Continued on page 118)

The Isle of the

By
ATWATER
CULPEPPER

Dead men under the sea, cannibal-corpses guarding the treasure of a mad priest who had been killed at the altar of his ghostly cathedral! Was the story true? A white girl and a young ship's-captain dare a cutthroat crew in this adventure on the floor of a south-sea lagoon

16

Restless Dead

Though their ear-drums were bursting, they watched those figures on the coral floor.

"FOR two years now, Captain McAndrew, I've been waiting —waiting for somebody to come along with the guts of a man! Somebody who isn't scared to death of ghosts swishing through the dark! Somebody who doesn't give a damn about corpses sunk under the cliffs—the restless dead! Why, over there on Motu Akua there's a fortune waiting for the man with nerve enough to come along and take it!"

Pete Mayo, new mate of the *Ghost*, slapped his knee in his excitement. Dick

McAndrew, lean, bronzed, hard-bitten, expelled a mouthful of smoke and spat over the rail.

"And you have me all sized up as that sort of man, Mr. Mayo? Thanks for the compliment. Heard that tale on the Papeete waterfront, didn't you? I've heard it myself—maybe a dozen times. That yarn had mold on it when Bougainville sailed these waters."

"But I *know!* I had it from a native who was dying—who had come from Motu Akua himself! Who couldn't stand it there any longer with the ghosts of the restless dead! The very island where Father Mathias lived fifty years ago! A cathedral whose very walls are covered with pearl-shell! And a fortune in pearls hidden in their burial place! Why, damn it, captain, it ain't more than a hundred miles off your course—two hundred at the most! It would make us—make you—rich for the rest of our lives!"

The mate bit through his pipestem in his excitement. Captain McAndrew tamped his tobacco and slowly lit his briar.

"I've no objection to being made rich for life," he drawled. "And ghosts, especially those of dead natives, never did worry me very much. In fact, I'd a damn' sight sooner meet a lot of those birds dead than alive. But down in the hold is a cargo of copra that I agreed to get to Papeete about as soon as I could make the trip. And there's a passenger—as you know."

Mayo's lip curled. "Hell with passengers! She can wait! We aren't running any speed boats out here among the islands!"

"Well—Miss Shearoyd figures to get back to the States without any more delay than she can help. No, mister, I don't feel any urge to go roving off my course on any wildcat pearl hunt—not now. This schooner has got business to attend to—and so has her captain."

"Playin' safe, eh, captain? You didn't use to have that reputation around the Islands."

"I play safe when I feel like it. And I'm still master of this ship. If you don't like your job, you can get off at the first island we touch. You were glad enough to get any kind of job when I found you—on the beach at Raro-Taro —even if you do have master's papers."

The mate flushed sullenly. "You don't have to rub it in, captain. I couldn't help it if my ship piled ashore in a hurricane, and left me out of a job!"

"Well, you brought it up yourself. And I'm telling you one more thing, mister. You watch your compass when you're on deck. If I find the schooner's getting off her course—I'll knock hell out of you!"

The younger man slouched forward sullenly. "Damn' careful about a *vahine!*" he muttered under his breath. "Well, this voyage ain't over yet!"

THE lean captain's eyes followed him. Mayo and the three new Kanaka sailors that he had taken on at Raro-Taro—he wondered, now. But the *Ghost* had been so terribly short-handed—

His rubber-soled shoes made no noise as he descended the companion-way. The girl, writing at a tiny table, hastily huddled her kimono about her bare shoulders.

"I didn't hear you, Captain McAndrew. It was stifling in the cabin—and I didn't think anybody'd come in here—"

McAndrew's eyes twinkled. "Keep your shirt on, Miss Shearoyd. I'm going into my own cabin to look over some charts."

The girl's eyes flared momentarily. Then a sense of humor came to her rescue. "I don't wear one, captain. Hadn't you found that out by this time?"

"I thought you knew me well enough by this time to know that women—white, cream, brown ones—don't mean a damn to me!"

"I wonder," Velma Shearoyd thought to herself. She moved imperceptibly— the blue kimono fell away from her rounded throat. His eye was drawn as if by a magnet to the upper hemispheres that rose from her narrow brassiere, the suggestion of a smooth valley between them, the soft white flesh below, encircled by a blue yoke—

His glance went resolutely to the open skylight. A faint smile played about her lips. The kimono fell farther open.

"Did you hear what that fool mate was proposing to me?"

"I couldn't very well help it. And you're willing to pass it up—because I want to get home?"

"You ready to fall for that yarn, too?"

"Tell me more about it!" The kimono had fallen back now. Nothing under it but the scanty brassiere, and the briefest of step-ins below whose lace cuffs her bare, creamy legs were crossed, her heelless slippers all but dropping off her pink toes.

"Why," he drawled, "that yarn's one of those that are bandied around the islands till you hear it so often you're ready to believe it yourself. It seems about fifty years ago there was a priest out on Motu Akua—Father Mathias, they called him. Queer sort of guy. A little cracked, maybe. One of those human dynamos who wouldn't spare himself or anybody else. Anyway, he had a hold on the natives that nobody's had before or since. He made converts—lots of them."

SHE bent forward, eyes gleaming. The kimono had all but slipped from her shoulders.

"Well, he set himself to build a cathedral—the finest one in the South Seas. He lashed the natives to such a superstitious pitch that they fairly wore themselves out, building the church for him. Big chiefs, head-hunters, *ariki,* working side by side with the warriors and the women. They carved big blocks of coral and dragged 'em up the beach —stewed till they dropped under the sun. Put up big pink and white walls, with spires far above the tallest palms.

"Pearls were plenty along the shores of that island—plenty as the sands in the sea. And they meant little or nothing to those islanders. Just something that glittered and looked pretty.

"Then, just as the mad priest had finished the work of building his cathedral —the very day he was about to dedicate it—he dropped dead at the altar. They were going to eat him—cut him up in pieces and bake him in banana-leaves— hope'd they'd get some of his qualities by doing it. Maybe they did. Maybe they dropped him out into the water, to prevent that same thing. Probably that's where Father Mathias is now."

Drops of perspiration stood out on the girl's white shoulders. She shivered despite the stifling heat of the cabin.

"Well, the natives died off by hundreds—thousands, even. For what good, they asked themselves. What had it all brought them? White man's clothes, prayers they didn't understand, white man's diseases—

"By night they thought they heard the wailing of the mad priest in the shrine —that it was filled with specters of the men who gave their lives to build it. The ghostly swishing of the thin-lipped priest in the vestments, smoldering fires in his gray eyes. They would not stay on the island with the souls of the restless dead. First one went, then others, scrambling to get away in their canoes. Some died of disease, some of—terror, maybe.

"Then they were all gone. All but the spirits of the dead—and the fortune in pearls. That's Motu Akua—the Isle of the Restless Dead."

"And that fortune is there—for the taking." She was on her feet in her excitement. The kimono lay over the chairback.

"Who knows?" McAndrew, too, had risen. "Are you, too, going to advise me to be damned fool enough to go wildgoosing after a native's yarn?"

The roll of the schooner sent her lurching toward him. His bronzed arm slid about her, the sinewy muscles tightened about her bare flesh. The soft, alluring warmth of her nearness acted like fire on his pent-up emotions.

His lean, bronzed hand smoothed her ivory bosom, slid down upon rounded globes that were only half-hidden by the narrow brassiere. He could feel them quiver under his hand, lift, all but burst from their fragile covering. A hook snapped. Impatiently she flung the dangling brassiere from her exquisite shoulders.

Her full, bare breasts were crushed against the thin cotton of his singlet. His arm slid down the velvety muscles of her back, under the silken yoke about her waist. She clung closer to him, every nerve afire—

Captain McAndrew almost pushed her away in a surge of self-renunciation. "Don't let me forget that you're my passenger, lady! And I've got to look over some charts." He swung about on his heel and slammed the door of his own cabin.

UP ON deck Pete Mayo brooded. The hard-boiled, adventurous Dick McAndrew—bah! Hard-boiled, was he? Dispose of him—seize the schooner—take the white *vahine*—go after the treasure—he could live like a king afterwards, despotic lord of some wave-washed island—

Velma Shearoyd flung herself face downward on her bunk, as nearly naked as the veriest native girl in her *pareu*. Every tense muscle was aflame—her rounded breasts faintly reddened by the pressure of the captain's fingers. Didn't care for women, did he? She set her teeth grimly. He hadn't deceived her.

Her lovely bare legs kicked angrily. She lay there while dusk deepened to darkness. She could hear the patter of naked feet on the deck above, the creak of pulley, the flap of canvas.

The schooner reeked with the sweetish overpowering scent of copra, of palm-oils, of frying fish, of ripening fruit. Above the slap of the waves came the monotonous, high-pitched chant from the native sailors forward, the strains of a wheezy accordion. Her eyes closed.

She woke to find the cabin pitch dark, its stuffiness unbearable. In a set of sheer voile pajamas she crept out on deck.

The sea was a vast bowl of heat, streaked by phosphorescent flashes. Above the creak of cordage, the gentle swish of the waves, she could hear a grating, tinny, rhythmic series of notes. On the deck lay Captain McAndrew's wheezy little phonograph, an old and scratched record revolving with irritating persistency.

"Karoni! You fella watch him *aveia* goddam close!"

THE captain was bending over the faintly lit compass. At the wheel

He whirled, but—Too late! The
silent figures were upon them.

stood a gigantic, almost nude brown
helmsman. "Watch him *niru*," McAndrew directed curtly, pointing to the
needle. He pulled a flat bottle from his
hip pocket and took a long pull.

"The last time I heard that—" she
pointed to the phonograph—"was on Tim
Burgoyne's island—a brown girl dancing
to it on the sand—"

His eyes lit with remembrance. "She

could dance, couldn't she? Pretty little
wild cat, wasn't she?"

"Would you like me to imitate her?
Dance most of my clothes off—as she
did?" The flame of her eyes matched the
phosphorescence of the sea overside.

His sneering laugh rang out harshly
above the lapping waves. "You! You
back-in-the-states women with your
small-town ideas of life! Why—you

wouldn't have the guts to do a thing like that! In the second place, you couldn't! It's born in these native girls!" He took a long pull at the bottle, and stared insolently at the girl in her pajamas.

"Some time, you domineering, scornful, sneering—I'll show you! Maybe I'll develop the—the—well, what you put so elegantly—"

"Intestinal fortitude," he prompted.

"The—guts—to do just that!"

He laughed uproariously. "I'll hold you to that—some time!"

He turned over the record. The notes of the phonograph were less metallic now. Involuntarily her bare feet glided about the rolling deck. She swayed, bent —his eyes lost their scornful disdain. "Why—you *can* dance!" he applauded grudgingly.

She flashed a smile at him. The spell of the moonlight seized her. She was borne back to that moment on the sands of Varo-Varo, another dancer—

As if hypnotized, she whisked her pajama top off, glided toward him, away, her naked breasts rising and falling—she swayed toward him—shoved at the elastic at her waist—

Dick McAndrew caught her hungrily in his arms.

The music died away to a scratchy squawk. Her bare arms were about his neck, tightening. . . .

A crouching figure in soiled whites crept noiselessly across the deck. McAndrew whirled, too late. A grim muzzle pressed into his ribs, a cunning, fanatic face—

Three silent, naked brown figures leaped out of the shadows upon the giant helmsman. Knives flashed in the moonlight—

FOR four days the little boat had drifted at the capricious mercy of wind and wave. Four days under blazing, mocking tropic sun, over long, lazy, spray-tipped swells that slapped at them and tossed them, this little craft with its two occupants.

It would have been a quicker, more merciful end, if Mayo's pistol had spat in the darkness—if he had tossed the lean body overboard for the sharks. But there was grim cruelty in his makeup— an aversion to direct bloodshed; he was very sure that the captain would never survive to reach land. And, much as he wanted to enjoy the charms of the white *vahine,* his hold over the Kanakas was none too sure.

They insisted with voluble gibbering that it was bad medicine to have a woman aboard.

With ill-concealed reluctance he had set Velma Shearoyd into the boat and watched the little craft from the deck of the schooner as it bobbed, a tiny speck, far away in the distance.

It had been the irony of fate that the little skiff had drifted under the searing and capricious winds, upon the very shores of Motu Akua. That Mayo's crude idea of where the treasure island lay had been several hundred miles out of the way. That, high above the palms, the fantastic spires of pink coral stretched toward an azure sky, on an island long ago deserted—the Isle of the Restless Dead.

A ghostly island. A land whose struggle was over. A treasure-chest of pearls in whose richness had lived a people content with lazy poverty till they were spurred from their lotus life by the blazing fanaticism of the ascetic priest, who had found death in his building an exotic temple for the glory of his faith.

THE two castaways crept silently into the shadowy recesses of the ghost cathedral. Magnificent in its original splendor, it was eerily grand in its ruin. Through the rotted holes in the roof, vagrant beams of sunlight served but to intensify the shadows.

At the very end of the damp, icily clammy temple a beam of sunlight fell upon a vast altar, iridescent and dazzling, covered every inch with nacre. Ironically a gigantic pearl cross, fallen and crumbled, lay sprawled across the altar top, as if in mockery of the mad priest, standing in his brilliant vestments, his arms outstretched at the very moment of his triumph.

They crept out noiselessly from the eerie cathedral. Out in the blazing sunlight they stopped and looked around the deserted village. Drops of perspiration stood out on Dick McAndrew's tanned shoulders. He wiped his forehead nervously.

"God!" he muttered, half to himself, half to the girl by his side. "Things have *happened* here!"

They found a hut, larger and less ruined than the others, that might well have been the residence of the mad priest. McAndrew brought ashore the few meager belongings they had been permitted to take with them, and set about making the wreck passably habitable.

The sun dropped, a glaring ball of fire, across the distant horizon. Darkness succeeded daylight almost without intermission.

It took the utmost of their fortitude to enter the grim silence of the deserted hut. McAndrew had matches—there were a few fragments of half-burnt and insect-chewed candles. He lit one, stuck it in a corroded candlestick, and let its flickering light cast deeper, more sinister shadows about the deserted interior.

"Puts you pretty much in the native frame of mind," he commented. "You can't blame those birds for believing in a spirit world only a hair's breadth from their own. Don't wonder that they walked in daily terror of the *akua-akuas.*"

"*Akua-akuas*—what are those?"

"The restless dead." His eyes tried to pierce the depths of a particularly sinister shadow. "Well, let's turn in. Got to save these candles. When they're gone—there won't be any more."

VELMA sat down upon the edge of the remade bed and began unfastening her dress. She pulled it off over her head, bent over and unfastened her garters, peeled down her stockings. McAndrew stood gazing at her with an inscrutable look in his eyes.

The flickering candle outlined the highlights of her rounded arms, the ivory columns of her thighs, her slim, delectable ankles. She bent over, slid the stocking over her bare toes, not quite daring to look into his eyes. Her heart thudded under the narrow brassiere. She straightened up at last.

McAndrew had turned away. He was going into the other room, swinging the sagging door to as far as it would go. She could hear him stumbling around in the darkness—the creak at last as he flung himself upon a rickety cot. She had looked forward to this moment ever since they had landed on the rocky shore, partly with apprehension, partly with another feeling that she could not analyze. She felt cheated—let down—

The candle was guttering low, a wavering trickle of smoke rising like sinister incense. Those shadows—from almost every one she could feel a ghostly presence peering, gibbering. Chiefs, whose bearded faces, whose filed teeth—who ate men—her white shoulders shook with terror she could not face alone.

She flung off the last of her undergarments, and crowded on her thin pajamas. The musty, dank smell of the deserted house—the stub of candle guttered, flickered eerily in a spreading pool of grease—then went out. She wanted to scream at the sudden darkness.

She crept softly over to the door, tugged at it as silently as she might, until it was wide open. She crept back in the darkness peopled with ghostly fears, and slipped into the makeshift bed, to lie there with eyes wide open.

The wind swished mournfully over the cliffs, over the coral-fringed lagoon, over the dead village—the cold wind, she told herself, that is born in lonely graveyards.

She was alone—with the *akua-akuas*, in the dark—the ghosts of the restless dead—who had died under the lash of fanatic urge. Alone—save for the man whose heavy breathing in the next room partly reassured her. The sobbing, moaning wind rose—

SHE woke reeking with clammy perspiration. It seemed that she could hear agonized wailings from the crumbled shrine, barely a stone's throw away. A blurry shadow that took form, lit by a ghastly purple glow, a spectral figure in ghostly vestments.

Smoldering fires shone in the gray eyes, set deep in a fleshless face. One hand held an iridescent cross—the other, long, bony, spectral fingers, was outstretched, extending toward her, hovering over her. Was it the sobbing wind in the palm-fronds, or was it real, a guttural croaking, that she heard—

"*Benedicite, mei filii—*"

She could not control the hoarse scream that welled from her throat.

"Dick! Oh, Dick!"

He was coming, stumbling through the darkness. His arms were about her, holding her tightly, reassuringly. Her arms were clasped about his neck, every taut muscle pressed tightly against him.

"Dick—don't—don't leave me! I'm —afraid!"

He didn't.

IN THE morning sunlight the placid waters of the lagoon were almost like a lake. Deep velvety shadows spread from the base of the cliffs, where the waves barely lapped. From the flat top that overhung the sea the castaways looked down to the crystal-clear water perhaps twenty feet below.

The rocks rose abruptly from a tiny beach on which, above tidemark, lay the skiff that had brought them to Motu Akua. Velma leaned over the rocks and peered into the glassy depth.

"I wonder what's down there. And what a place to dive! If I could do it the way Ranoa did—at Vanuhiva—"

McAndrew shrugged his bronzed shoulders under his thin singlet. "If you practiced, year in and year out, the way they do—"

Velma sat down on the rock. She peeled down her stockings, sat momentarily wriggling her bare toes in the blaze of the sunlight. Her fingers went to the fastenings of her dress, undid them— she whipped the gown over her creamy shoulders, and stood on the ledge, poised against the sunlight, a lovely alluring figure in the briefest and wispiest of blue step-ins.

"What in the devil?" demanded the astonished McAndrew.

She leaped in the clean-cut parabola from the edge of the cliff. Even Ranoa, the native diving-girl at Vanuhiva, could not have done it better. She cut the blue-green water at the base of the cliff without the vestige of a splash, went down, down into the cool depths—

Fascinated, McAndrew watched from the edge of the cliff. A tinge of uneasiness crept over his face. Then, reassured, he saw the creamy form float upward, come to the surface, and strike out toward the little beach. He scram-

Even as the brown man staggered the cross descended in a crushing blow.

bled down over the rocks to meet her.

He was unprepared for the horror in her eyes. Stark, wide open, terror-stricken, as one who has looked on things that should not be seen.

"I saw them—they're there!" she panted. "The *akua-akuas!* The restless dead! They moved! They pointed at me!"

His arm went around the wet white flesh and drew her trembling form tightly to him. "Nonsense! You've gone just a little balmy—too much exposure—alone on this ghastly island—"

"But I did see them!" she persisted. She shivered, she clutched at him and would not let him go. "A row of dead men—standing there under the cliff—all in a rank—with white *pareus*—"

He held her tightly in his arms, smoothing her wet, white body, the dripping silk that clung tightly to her lovely hips, the rippling muscles of her satin back.

"You don't believe it!" She had freed herself, was running up the cliff, stood poised on the edge of the rock. Again she leaped in a clean-cut dive.

McAndrew flung off his trousers, and leaped after her. Down, down the two figures went. And as McAndrew opened his eyes under water, he all but choked as he swam over to the girl's taut figure. He forgot everything but the ghostly conclave before him till his bursting lungs forced him to seek the surface again.

STANDING in ranks on the coral floor in the opal water was a ghostly array of men. They had been men—once. Upright against the face of the submerged cliff, silent and dead in the seaweed, their white loin cloths knotted about them like belts of stone.

Petrified by some mysterious action of water and coral, as lifelike as the day their dead bodies had been lowered into the waves to their watery burial, to cheat those who would eat them in religious fanaticism—would cut them into jagged hunks of flesh and stew them in the cooking-pots sacred to long-pig.

Their very eyes, hardened to glass, seemed to roll, to blink, to follow every movement of the daring intruders who broke in upon the quiet of their under-sea graves.

And in the center stood a whiter figure than those of the brown chieftains. A form in purple vestments—the mad, ascetic Father Mathias, who had joined the last resting-place of his converts in the waters of the lagoon. His thin, fleshless face, his glassy eyes far back in the bony sockets, peering out from the recesses of a stony cowl, seemed to glare solemnly at them—was it a grim smile that seemed to be fixed on those thin lips, tightly set in death?

The dead priest's arm seemed to move solemnly, majestically, by some freak of the eddying current, as if bestowing some ghostly benediction upon the ranks of his dead followers. Was it the swish of the waves, or could their bursting ear-drums almost hear the *"Ben' dicite, me' fil'—"*

The bony, outstretched arm beckoned, swung, seemed to clutch at the swimmers—knotty, thin fingers clawed toward them—

The two lay panting on the little beach, clasped in each other's arms. Velma clung tightly to him, her wet arms about his neck, her dripping limbs pressed against his thighs. Her warm, wet body seemed to be a part of him. "It's—it's true—about the mad priest!" she gasped. "He—he wants us—"

Reluctantly McAndrew disengaged himself. His keen eyes had caught a glimpse of something in the middle of the ghostly conclave. He dived again from the cliff, down again among the dead men.

Shuddering he felt swiftly around the corpses, pried a coral-encrusted casket loose from its resting-place.

They opened it far up on the cliffs. In the blazing sunlight poured out a cascade of iridescent globules, that gleamed enticingly as they scooped up handfuls. Pearls of a size and luster that surpassed the wildest dreams of the avaricious pearler.

"Rich—rich for life!" McAndrew gasped, as he surveyed the glittering treasure.

"But—what good will they do us?" Velma sighed at last.

What good? Over on the other side of that rim of waters they would spell wealth—luxury—a millionaire's treasure. On this deserted island, where ships never came—now and then a bank of lights against the night, at long intervals, a streamer of smoke on the horizon. But no one ever stopped there who did not have to.

FAR across the horizon the notched pinpoint that broke the skyline grew larger. It was setting directly toward their island. With beating hearts the two castaways stood on the cliffs of Motu Akua and watched the vessel beat nearer.

Suddenly McAndrew caught the girl's hand and drew her down flat upon the rock. "God!" he breathed, as if fearful that his voice would carry across the distant water. "I'd know that foresail anywhere! It's the last ship in the world I want to see in these waters! It's the *Ghost!*"

It was the *Ghost*. The schooner tacked toward the island, circled around the surf-fringed barrier, and came on steadily through the one opening in the reef. With tightened lips, crouching on the cliff, they watched the patched foresail drift nearer.

Bending low, fearful lest they be seen through the binoculars, they crept along the ledge and into the hut that had served Father Mathias for a home. It was too late to seek the interior of the island, even if that would have served them. They would surely be discovered in flight. Weaponless—

McAndrew caught up the corroded casket and dragged the girl after him. "Into the cathedral!" he cried. "It's our only chance! If I know these Kanakas—"

They could hear the shrill shouts of the native crew, the rattle of the anchor-chain, Mayo's stentorian oaths as he urged his crew ashore.

They had over-run the village, running with savage cries in and out of the deserted huts. They were swarming over the threshold of the deserted rectory, overturning everything—

Mayo's bullying tones came clearly to their ears. "Hell! Someone's livin' here! That fire hasn't been out more'n an hour! You fella, ketchum!"

McAndrew dragged the girl down behind the deserted altar.

There was some hitch. Bluster and swear as he might, Mayo could not induce his superstitious natives to enter the deserted church.

His lone figure strode through the sagging doors, blinked for a moment as he came in from the bright sunlight. As his eyes accustomed themselves to the gloom, he shouted involuntarily at sight of the shell-covered walls, the nacre-encrusted altar.

"Shell enough to make a man rich for life! Was I right? Now if I could only find them damn' pearls—"

He strode toward the altar and kicked inquiringly at the shell that covered it. A fragment fell from one corner, struck the girl's shoulder cruelly, so that she winced.

Faint as was her involuntary gasp, Mayo's keen ears heard it. He whipped

(Continued on page 107)

Cats of

Her unearthly beauty was a snare to the wicked
—her eerie companions were as weird as the
fortune-teller herself . . . a slinking horde
to suck the hot blood of death at last.

THEY came at him like a soft, furry avalanche, so that he would have cried out had not some strange paralysis glued his tongue. From the doors they came, and from the dark corners. On softly-padded feet they sprang at him, silently like black ghosts, their green eyes glowing lambent fire. They were as creatures from hell, and their number was unending. Without

Cassandra

By
ELLERY
WATSON
CALDER

"You need not fear," the vision said;
"they will do you no harm."

sound and without warning they appeared; they were a dark tide of living movement, and they came toward him.

He shrank backward from their advance, and a great fear filled him. He found the door through which he had entered, and he fumbled at the knob. Then cold moisture beaded his forehead, and trembled with a sudden, nauseating terror; for the door was strangely locked, so that he could not flee.

The furry, silent horde was close to him now. A gulping sob rasped within his constricted throat, and dread panic seized at his heart. Like a nightmare it seemed to him—the gloom-veiled, sinister house, the unlocked door that had invited his entrance, the sudden realization that he was trapped. Yet it was real—horribly real. The house was real; the oncoming, silent avalanche was real. Green eyes burned into his brain.

And then, at a far doorway, there was suddenly Cassandra.

She spoke a command; and her voice was like a deep-throated purr. At her bidding, the furry tide halted.

She smiled at Mort Marriner. "You are afraid of my cats?" she asked him quietly.

He found his voice. It trembled strangely in his throat. "I—yes, I was—afraid—"

"You need no longer fear. They will do you no harm." She came toward him, and her movement was silent, with a feline grace.

HE tore his eyes away from the furry things at his feet, and his gaze rested upon the girl who drew near to him. The garment that covered her was a flowing thing of some queer, almost translucent material that shimmered greenly in the semi-dark. Through it he could discern the smooth, catlike litheness of her body, and the rounded promonitories of her breasts.

He looked into her eyes, and his own grew wide with wonderment. Her pupils were dark vertical slits in irises of green, and it seemed to him that her eyes glowed strangely in the gloom. She smiled once more, and her white teeth were pointed and sharp with a feline sharpness.

Abruptly he knew that he was afraid of her.

It was as though she had divined his fear, for she said, "I mean you no harm. I would only ask what you want of me."

Her long, white-tapered hands hung at her sides. He saw the crimson splashes that were her sharp fingernails, and they reminded him of claws that had been dipped deep in blood. . . He shuddered, and his mind sought for a plausible excuse for his being in that somber house.

Then he remembered the dim sign outside. In the baleful white gleam of the full moon he had read it: "Madame Cassandra, Seeress." Now he licked his parched lips. He dared not tell her that he had found her front door unlocked; that he had entered silent and unbidden, with robbery in his heart. Instead, he croaked a craven's lie. "I—my name's Mort Marriner. I came here to see Madame Cassandra to have my fortune told. I rang the bell, but no one answered. Then I found the front door unlocked, and came in."

The girl in shimmering green smiled softly. "You wish Madame Cassandra to read your future?" she purred in her flawless throat.

"Yes. Is—is she in?" Desperately he hoped that her answer would be negative, so that he could leave this place.

The girl said, "I am Cassandra."

He stared at her, for the moment confused. "But—you are too young—!"

"I am Cassandra," she repeated. She touched his arm, and a cold wind seemed to blow through the crevices of his mean soul. "Come," she said slowly. "Come with me."

Unwillingly he followed her, back into a smaller room where green lights flickered ghoulishly. And although he did not look back, he knew that the furry horde was at his heels—silent, watchful, like flitting shadows.

In a huge chair Cassandra seated herself, so that the flickering green lights were reflected in her strange eyes. On the table before her was a huge crystal in which the green lights danced deeply, like imprisoned ghosts of fire. Green lights and green eyes and flickering green fires seared deep into Mort Marriner's brain, and his hands were cold.

He felt a furry thing rub against his leg, and sharp claws bit at his flesh suddenly. He cried out, in a voice loud with terror. Cassandra smiled and spoke in a strange, slurred tongue that he did not, could not comprehend.

Then her gaze flickered across his corpse-white features, and her purring tone was warm-reassuring. "I have told them that you are my friend. They understand now, and will not alarm you more."

He tried to answer her; tried to tell her that he no longer sought a forecast of his future. He tried to tell her that he wanted, desperately, to leave. But once more that strange paralysis locked his tongue, and he was silent.

Cassandra's cat eyes went dreamily to the green-glowing crystal. It was as though he had not been there with her in the room.

LONG she stared into the gleaming globe; and there seemed to be a purring sound deep in her throat. Her black hair streamed down over her shoulders like an inky waterfall, and her breasts were perfect beneath the translucence of her shimmering emerald garment. And then, dreamily, she spoke as though from a far, distant place.

"The story of Cassandra is a story of tragedy," she said slowly.

"Of—of Cassandra?" Mort Marriner spoke the words thickly.

"Cassandra was daughter to Priam, King of Troy. She was the beloved of Apollo, who gave to her the gift of prophesy. Love is a strange thing, my friend. Apollo's died. He became angry with Cassandra. And because he could not take from her the gift of prophesy which he had bestowed upon her, he decreed a bitter thing. He decreed that henceforth no living man should believe the things she prophesied." The girl sighed gently. Cassandra was killed, afterward, in the sacking of Troy."

Mort Marriner wiped the cold moisture from his forehead, and his question was thick-tongued. "But—what has that to do with me?" he choked.

"Only this, my friend. The things I see within this crystal are things that will inevitably come to pass; and yet you will not believe them."

"You—see things in the crystal?" He stared into the gleaming iridescent globe, but his eyes encountered naught save flickering, imprisoned green lights. . .

"I see many things in the crystal," she answered. "I see that you came here to rob me, because you had heard whisperings of the treasure I possess."

"It's—it's—" He tried to tell her it was a lie, but the untruth lodged in his throat and would not utter. He was silent and abruptly ashamed. And he was frightened with a nameless dread.

Her green eyes swept his face, and then they returned to the emerald-gleaming crystal ball. "There are ominous things in store for you, Mort Marriner," she said. "And . . . for me. Yet before these events come to pass there will be a brief moment of intoxication—of rapture—"

"I—I don't want to hear any more!" he cried out.

"But you will hear until the end, Mort Marriner. You will stay, and you will hear, because it has been written thus since time began."

"God!" he whispered.

Again she gazed deep into the crystal. "I see strange things," she purred huskily. "I see—" abruptly her voice choked off, and her face went white. She pushed the crystal globe from her, and her crimson-tipped fingers trembled strangely. She arose, and the grace of her body was feline, cat-like. Her hand went to her breast, pressed into the firm-resilient flesh through the translucent stuff of her robe as though to still a sudden beating of her heart. And as Mort Marriner's fascinated eyes followed her gesture, he suddenly lost all fear.

Instead, there surged up within him a desire for her that licked at his veins like green fire. It was queer, he thought, that his terror of her should thus be transformed into desire; yet it must have been inevitably so, for she was beautiful with a weird and unearthly beauty that transcended mortal perfection.

Her mouth was crimson-ripe with kisses to be harvested, and her body was made for the embrace of passion. Her hips were sinuously curved, and her bosoms were twin dreams that cried out for his caresses. One step he took toward her.

SHE smiled into his eyes, and her hand brushed his arm. This time it was no cold wind that froze the crevices of his soul, but a hot gusty storm that filled him with aching and longing.

"Come, Mort Marriner," she said. "I will show you the treasure you had hoped to steal."

And now he followed her willingly, eagerly; nor did he think of the pad-padding, furry things that flowed like a living tide at his heels. She led him up a dim stairway, and they entered a perfumed room.

She went to a grotesque-carven chest. As though by some magic its lid flew up at her touch.

Her blood-red fingers dipped into the chest's interior, and when she withdrew her hands they were draped with scintillant gems that glistened and glittered and gleamed. There were diamonds and rubies as red as warm-flowing blood, and there were emeralds that glowed green like the eyes of a cat . . . like the eyes of Cassandra. At the sight of them Mort Marriner drew his breath, painful-sharply.

And then he knew that he had no desire for the jewels; knew that this girl in the green translucent garment was the only thing in that dim house that he wanted. He went to her, and his hands disentangled the ropes of gems from her fingers so that they slid back glisteningly into the chest, with tiny clatter-noises.

She faced him, and very slowly he reached up to unfasten the shimmering robe where it was caught together at her neck. A light flared into her eyes as the sleazy drape rippled to the floor. Then she stood before him in glorious nakedness, and reverently he drank in the glories of her body with his eyes.

He touched her, suddenly fearful that so much perfection be not real. Her flesh was warm to his fingers; her breasts

The knife stuck horribly in her throat, mocking him as he picked up the jewels.

throbbed like captive things beneath his palms. He kissed her.

She fused against his body like a vibrant reed, and he could feel the quivering tremble of her in his hard arms. Then he picked her up gently, although his veins seethed and bubbled with hot passion; and he kissed her neck, her shoulders, as though he had been long-starved for the taste of her flesh. . .

By some necromancy they were to-gether upon a cushioned divan, silk-soft and passion-warm. Her arms were about his neck, and her blood-red lips parted once more for his ardent-questing kiss.

He felt the tip of her tongue; *it was rough, scratchy, like a cat's!*

Abruptly a cold, wintry chill seemed to freeze his marrow, and he stared into her green-irised eyes that were like a cat's eyes. She smiled, and her sharp-pointed teeth were like cat's teeth. Her black hair had fallen away from her face, and as he saw her ears he felt suddenly sick, then suddenly red-raging. *Her ears were soft and furry and pointed—like cat's ears!*

He could not fathom the abrupt fury that surged in him; could not plumb the insane and frenetic fear that made him leap up from her warm side. It was as though he had gone out of his body, and a raging demon had entered. As though in an anger-ridden nightmare he felt his hand go to the knife at his belt, saw the blade glitter in the dim light as he brought it plunging down into the white flesh of her throat. . .

AND then he came to his senses, and flung the intruding demon from him. Like waves beating against his brain came the reiterated knowledge, over and over a thousand times. He had killed Cassandra, and she was dead.

He looked at her, and then he closed his eyes weakly. The knife still quivered in her warm throat, and red blood streamed over the cushioned divan, crimson-staining and murder-accusing.

Slowly he gripped himself; slowly and cautiously he edged away from her lovely lifeless corpse. He must get away, he said. He must escape, he told himself. He must leave this ghastly house, he whispered.

Why had he killed Cassandra? He did not know. He knew only that suddenly he had hated her; had hated her feline body and her cat's eyes and furry, pointed ears with a consuming hatred. It was as though his hatred had been a thing apart from him—predestined from the beginning of time. . .

"It has been written thus since time began"—that was what Cassandra had told him, when she had looked into the green-glowing crystal. A cold sweat stood out on his forehead and made his body wet, cold. Was it this she had meant when she had predicted an hour of intoxication, of bliss, for them both—before ominous things overshadowed them?

He shook himself, forced himself to laugh aloud in that silent murder-room. He was being a fool! There need be nothing ominous ahead of him—if he was very careful. He would get away, go to some far place, forget this night of miasmatic nightmare. But . . . he had no money. How could he journey to a far place without money?

Then he smiled. Why had he come here in the first place? Because he had intended to steal Cassandra's jewels! Well, the carven chest was still open, and Cassandra had no further need of them—

He leaped to the chest, stuffed his pockets with the glittering baubles until his coat bulged pregnantly. Then, resolutely his eyes avoiding the bleeding thing on the divan, he left the room and stole softly down the stairs.

He reached the lower hall. He frowned. He had forgotten something. What was it? He could not remember. Then, suddenly he did remember.

He remembered because it was written since the beginning of time. And the thing he remembered was—that furry avalanche, fiery-eyed and silent-footed!

They were coming toward him. He would have cried out had not some strange paralysis glued his tongue. From the hallway they came, and from the dark corners. On softly-padded feet they sprang at him, silently like black ghosts, their green eyes glowing lambent fire. And then they were upon him.

He beat at them frantically, his terrified hands striking into their furry midst. Their sharp claws tore at his fingers, stripped the flesh from the bones of his wrists and arms. Their sharp feline teeth were at his legs, so that he could feel his hot life-blood draining from him.

He went to his knees in that silent feline welter. Needle-sharp claws lacerated his cheeks and sank gruesomely into his eyeballs . . .

Hell-blackness overtook him, and he died.

* * * *

From the Evening Bulletin, Feb. 15, 193—

FIND SKELETON IN HOUSE; WOMAN MISSING

Attracted by the strange yowling of cats, Patrolman Dennis Lafferty today forced his way into a house at 1677 N. Aldama Street and stumbled upon a gruesome find. In the lower hallway was the skeleton of a man, the flesh completely gone from the bones.

The house, which had been occupied by a woman known only as "Cassandra," a mystic and fortune-teller, was unoccupied except for a horde of black cats whose noise had attracted the policeman. Cassandra herself was not at home, and up until a late hour this afternoon had not been located by the police.

A strange factor in the mystery lies in the discovery, in a room on the second floor, of the body of a huge black cat. The animal was dead. It had a dagger in its throat.

MATE FOR

Snakes with feet . . . lizards with wings . . . men without arms—such were the doctor's mad creations! With a lovely girl in his power, what new horror did he plan?

THE odor was unforgettable, an odor like nothing else—the putrid, rotting smell of *mud*. Water glinted and glistened in the pale moonlight, shining between long streamers of Spanish moss which hung from the ghostly cypresses.

Swamp! Swamp on four sides, a bottomless quagmire, making the knoll on which the big house stood a veritable island in an unhealthy sea of viscous slime. The watcher at the window shrugged muscled shoulders before turning away from the moonlit ghastliness to drop on the bed.

In spite of the thick breeze, perspiration was heavy on his body. The air was fetid, charged. He lay there on his back staring up at the ceiling with bitter eyes, cursing the eccentricity of a world-famed surgeon who preferred to live in the midst of a swamp like a hermit—and saving a few words of profanity for a city editor who considered the rumor of a new surgical discovery news.

MEDUSA

By
CARL MOORE

Two hands held his wrists while a third went around his neck. The doctor turned to the girl.

Dr. Lombard had been too busy to see Martin, the reporter, on his arrival, but had proved hospitable to say the least. Martin hadn't minded the waiting; a good radio, a magazine, and a bottle of the doctor's best Scotch took the edge off the delay. But he eventually fell asleep hating the dank, eerie atmosphere arising from the swamplands about him.

He awakened suddenly, every nerve in his immense body quivering madly. Was that scream part of a nightmare? Again it came, the ear piercing shriek of an utterly terrified woman.

37

"Help! Help! Help!" followed by dry sobs of terror.

Trembling, Eddie Martin stumbled to the hall door, tugged at it in vain. Locked! Unbelievingly he felt for a key that was no longer there. Yet, *he distinctly remembered locking that door himself and leaving the key inside!*

Again that dreadful scream of fear and agony, coming definitely from beyond the nearest wall, from the very next room! He moved swiftly toward the locked connecting door, beat on it with clinched fists.

"Open up! Open up!" he bellowed. "Dr. Lombard! Dr. Lombard! I say in there—open up!"

The agonized scream again reverberated through the thickness of the swamp night. Martin reached for a heavy chair, meaning to crash the door open, and to his dumb amazement the chair failed to yield to his hand! It was fixed fast to the floor!

His square jaw sat a little more firmly as he retreated a few paces, flexed brawny shoulders. Like a football player he charged the barred door. Once, twice, three times, he hit it with all the power of two hundred and twenty pounds of bone, muscle, and sinew. The fourth time it gave, the lock yielding, the door swinging suddenly open.

Martin sprawled headlong, stumbled to a crouch, ready for he knew not what. Nothing stirred. The moon filtered through the steel screen to paint with white magic. He looked again before recognizing the still form on the bed for what it was—a woman.

SHE lay there bathed by moonlight, slender body statuesque, completely feminine. The torn remains of a silken gown were gathered at her waist revealing unadorned hips, tapering thighs that glistened and gleamed in the eerie light.

The dusty valley between her heaving breasts was shadowed, mauve in the moonlight; the crowned white mounds still trembled. Eyes were closed, arms stretched high. Martin looked twice before discovering they were tied to the head of the bed—tied roughly, crudely with strips of linen torn from the sheet that had once covered her slender body.

There was no mark to mar the unflecked perfection of her loveliness; the racing heart-beat burning through soft flesh into the palm of his questing hand proved she had merely fainted. A sweet, sickish smell lingered over all and the wadded rag Martin picked from the pillow was damp. He sniffed it suspiciously. Chloroform!

He beat at her hall door, only to find it, too, locked. He called Dr. Lombard's name until his lungs ached; all to no avail. The woman's moan on regaining consciousness brought him again to the bedside.

"It's all right," he soothed. "I'm a friend. Try to tell me what happened."

Eventually she grew calmer, although violet eyes were still wide with remembered terror. Even then her story was garbled, uncertain, hardly believable. Nightmare? Martin wondered. He caught himself sniffing cynically at her breath.

SHE had been awakened by a heavy body pressing her own slender loveliness to the bed, clamping the chloroformed rag against her mouth and nostrils, blinding her at the same time. Losing consciousness she had reawakened to find her arms tied to the rounds of the bed, to feel hot, fevered breath on her flesh and to cringe beneath the caress of a wet touch.

Not the touch of hands! The fumbling, passionate digits that swept across burning breasts, caressing the vibrant flesh, were not fingers. *They were toes!* The moon cast ample light to add to the girl's terror by revealing that the man fondling her body so hungrily was armless!

His hairy paleness had gleamed whitely in the moonlight; his shoulders were smooth, not even marred by the stumps of arms. As she told of the ghastliness of the touch of those pinching, probing toes she cradled her abused breasts in her own little hands, pressing them close as if to guard them from further indignities.

She sat in the middle of the bed, making no attempt in her fright to conceal her nudity, and Martin suddenly thought of his own scanty attire—an undershirt and shorts! Assuring her that he would return at once he made for his own room.

The light failed to respond to the switch but the moonlight, eerie and phosphorescent was sufficient. His bag and clothing were gone! He stood there for a moment cursing, more upset at the loss of his gun than anything else. Again he tried the hall door. It was locked.

He examined the window carefully. The heavy mesh of steel screen was secured on the outside by long iron strips. He was as safely imprisoned as if in a dungeon!

"My clothes!" gasped the girl in the moonlit doorway. "My clothes are gone!"

Imprisoned—the two of them—as safely and completely as if locked in the Bastille! Martin shrugged.

"Well," he grinned, speaking with a steadiness he failed to feel, "looks like we're to be here for some time. Let's sit down somewhere and see what happens next. Damned if I'm going to beat my hands off on locked doors again. Surely someone will let us out sooner or later. Something or other has gone wrong."

SHE sat close to him on the divan, shuddering from time to time as if in memory of the past few moments. Trying to soothe her while they waited for release, the man spoke quietly and softly, but his eyes were drawn to the curves and contours beneath the torn strips of silk.

"I'm Eddie Martin," he spoke gravely, "special writer on the *News*. The boss sent me down this evening to see Doc Lombard about some sort of new grafting process he's perfected. But doc was busy and asked me to stay over till tomorrow."

One confidence invited another.

"I'm Helen Vinton," she returned in a low voice, still gazing fearfully at the darker corners of the room. "I wasn't exactly asked down here, and I wish I hadn't come! Dr. Lombard is my brother-in-law."

"Oh!" Silence a moment while Martin tried to take his mind off the white expanse of tapering legs beside him, to pay stricter attention to the conversation. "Old doc married your sister? Well, where—"

To his infinite surprise she dropped her head to his sturdy shoulder and began to sob. Surprised? Certainly, but Eddie Martin never won a byline through failing to recognize opportunity. His arm slid about those trembling shoulders in the most approved manner and his hand rested in the most restable place!

"There, there," he soothed, patting her.

Presently she spoke, as a small, frightened child might speak to an adult.

"Mona and I were all that was left! And now she's gone, too!"

"Gone? Why what—?" The next second he kicked himself mentally.

"Dead!" Sobs wracked the slender body. "I didn't hear for months and months, and finally came out here to see for myself! Dr. Lombard showed me her grave. Oh, why couldn't he have let me known before? Why couldn't—?"

BANG! bang! bang! at the door. It crashed open, revealing a huge negro, lamp in hand. He peered in at them, grinning, and the crooked figure of Dr. Lombard appeared behind him.

"Good evening, my friends," he simpered, hobbling into the room.

"Listen, doc," Martin's voice was threatening, his arm still protectively about the rounded shoulders of Helen Vinton. "What's the idea of—?"

Movement arrested the angry words.

Both the doctor and his huge helper wore long Russian peasant blouses, sleeveless. Despite his deformed body, the doctor's arms were as muscled and tremendous as those of the six foot negro beside him. The negro, in turn, seemed somewhat deformed in the same manner as his master—not hunchbacked, but rather hunch-chested. It was as if the breast bones on both men had somehow been broken outward, making vee-shaped bulges. A long slot in the blouses ran straight down their respective breasts.

Something stirred and moved restlessly in that hump on the doctor! The negro put the lamp on the table, walked toward the opposite side of the room. Martin watched him from the corner of his eye, but the slimy movement beneath the fabric covering Lombard's chest excited more curiosity; the negro servant was behind him before he knew it.

"Listen, doc," Martin finally found his angry voice again, "what the hell happened to my clothes? And Miss Vinton here was attacked, I tell you! What kind of a joint—"

The doctor's upraised hand stopped him.

"No need to introduce you, I can see that!" The nastiness of his smile caused the woman to flush, caused Martin to begin an angry retort, only to be stopped again by that raised hand.

"My dear sister-in-law, I am very sorry that you disliked your experience. Yes, I know all about it. The attack, as you call it, was perpetrated by one of my very favorite patients—or perhaps experiments, is the better word. To be truthful, I rather planned it. You see I have evolved a little stimulant that makes a mere man seek the opposite sex in spite of the greatest of hindrances. I gave this favored patient of mine a little injection to note his reactions, and naturally he sought you, my dear! Quite complimentary, eh? And I can't say I blame him much!"

His eyes were bold, lascivious. She grasped the shreds of her torn gown closer to the mounds of her trembling breasts. Martin started forward angrily. Something seized him from behind. Two powerful brown hands grabbed his wrists with the pitiless tenacity of clamps. Pinioned for the moment he stood there motionless while Lombard continued his speech.

"Yes, my dear Helen, you are quite lovely indeed! Perhaps before you leave I can persuade you to take your dead sister's place for a few moments at least! Just as a penalty for your nosiness!"

Martin strained to break loose; the doctor gestured impatiently.

A GREAT, brawny arm shot round Martin's throat, tugged his head up and back, *while two brown hands never loosened their grip on his wrists!* He lashed out with his heels, all to no avail. The breath of the negro on his neck

The room began to haze before the girl's eyes, while the armless one came nearer.

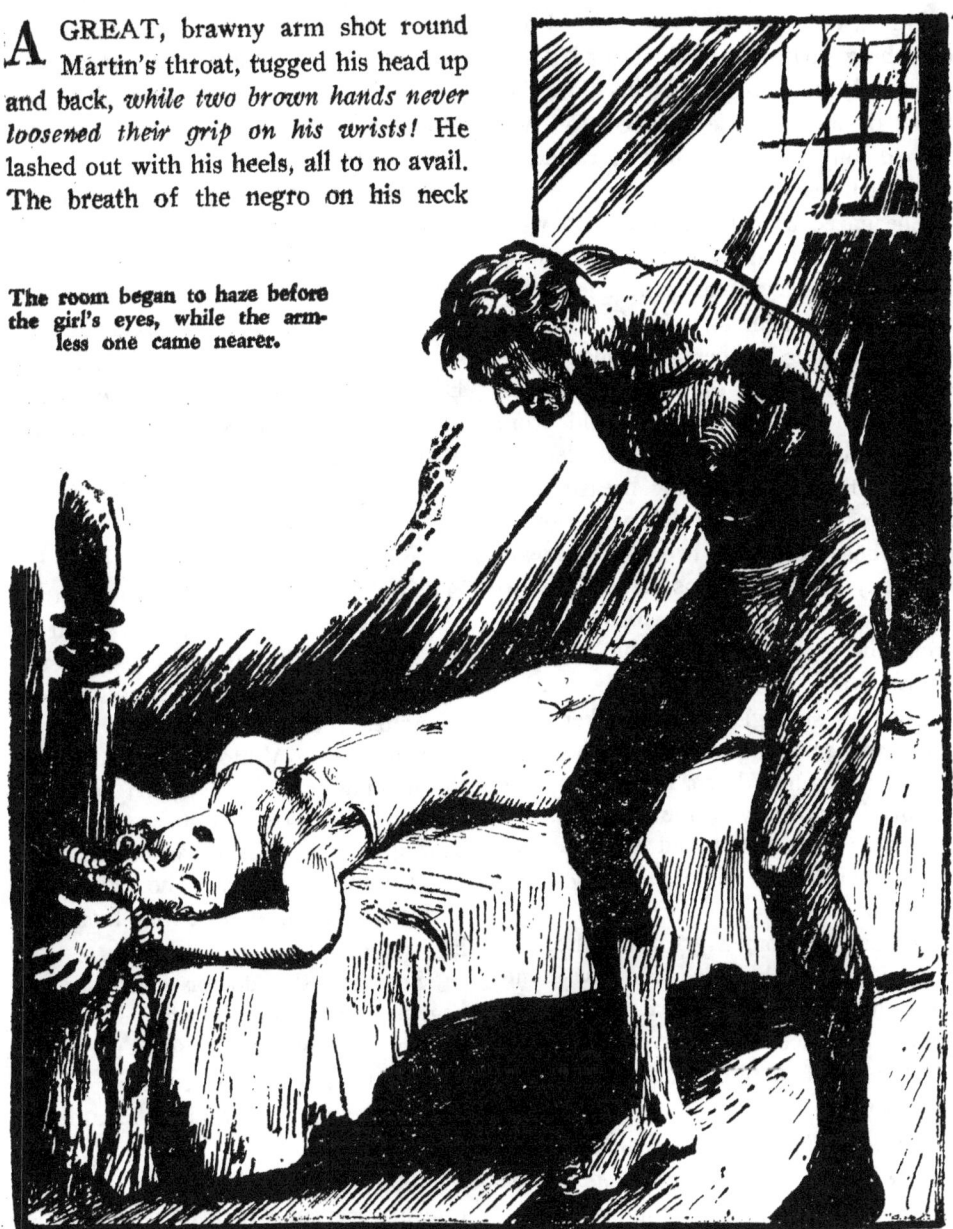

was quiet, almost unlabored. He held the two hundred-twenty pounds of athlete that was Martin as easily as a man holds a baby. Two hands at his wrists, one hand at his throat!

In his frantic twistings and turnings he caught sight of Helen Vinton crouched half-naked against the wall, her eyes wide with terror as she watched. The brawny arm beneath his chin pressed relentlessly tighter and tighter on his throat. His tongue swelled and emerged as he choked and panted, laboring and toiling for precious breath! The room began to haze before his bulging eyes.

He saw Lombard walk toward the crouching girl with catlike tread, long, powerful arms dangling at his sides like those of an ape. He reached for her, twined long fingers in her hair, jerked her cruelly erect.

She gazed at her torturer with wide eyes, too terrified to scream. He flung her to the table as easily as one would a doll, whipped the torn fabric from her body, exposing all her gleaming loveliness to his avid eyes. He giggled like a drunken man as his hand slid from her shoulder to cradle and sink deep in the soft flesh of her white breasts. Not in a caress, but in a terrible welt-raising grip whose very pain brought a scream of agony to her red lips, caused her to kick frantically and try to roll away from the cruel talon that bit into her tender flesh.

Martin's struggles grew weaker. The room rocked and trembled as the huge negro choked him down. His wrists were pinioned helplessly while the arm beneath his chin threatened to break his neck, strain as he might in the opposite direction.

Seemingly from a great distance the scream beat on his ears. He saw Lombard grasp the fair throat in his two hands, lean across her struggling body with his own to pin her flailing legs,—and then—

Through the slit in the front of Lombard's blouse crept another hand! A hand with twitching, grasping fingers, a hand attached to a hairy wrist which swelled to a muscular forearm! Two hands choking her relentlessly into submission—a third hand, from Lombard's bosom—creeping over her straining body up into the valley between her flattened breasts, fondling, caressing greedily!

Before unconsciousness took him Martin realized why his own frantic struggles were so fruitless. The negro who gripped him so tightly from behind also had three arms! A hand on each of his, Martin's, wrists, and another arm pitilessly beneath his chin!

He opened his eyes cautiously a few moments later to find the room in darkness. He sensed bodies close beside him, felt carpet beneath his bare shoulders, eventually realized his whereabouts. He lay on the floor in a black corner of Helen Vinton's room and beside him in the darkness crouched Lombard and the huge negro.

Men with three arms! Martin fought for his sanity.

MOONLIGHT slithered through the window to bathe a still form on the bed. Martin suppressed the start that would reveal his consciousness, recognizing that shapely figure as the body of Helen Vinton stretched out in the moonlight as he had first seen her, rounded arms tied to the head of the bed, generous, taut breasts rising and falling rhythmically. The whispered words of Lombard kept him from calling out in alarm.

"Sssssh!" the doctor cautioned the negro. "I hear him coming! I tell you, Harry my boy, that stuff is perfection itself. He can no more resist coming back to her than he can help breathing!"

Silence.

Hoping to free his bound wrists in time to prevent whatever was about to occur Martin toiled and strained in the darkness.

The slish of naked feet! A white figure, crouched like an ape, slunk in, gazed about him with mad eyes that reflected madder fires in the moonlight. The thing, breathing audibly, driveling, gibbering, stepped into the square of white moonlight by the bed. *He had no arms! No stumps of arms!* Merely smooth shoulders, as if arms had never been there!

A board creaked in the corner and the armless one cast wary eyes in their direction. Again Martin almost gasped, for in spite of the slush and the slime of the swamp, the peering features were recognizable! He knew this man! Carl Clauser! That was the name! But love of God! The man certainly had two arms when he worked beside him a year ago on the *News!* What had—?

Softly the armless one pattered to the bedside. He leaned over the unconscious beauty of Helen Vinton and tiny, cottony drops of drooling saliva flecked her body from his slathering lips. He trembled and shook under some terrible stress. He leaned across the woman and gloated for a moment, his breath quickening at the sight of those lush, palpitant breasts.

Just as the horrified Martin started to call his name the armless one jerked suddenly erect, sank half-sitting, half reclining on the bed beside the unconscious girl.

His feet shot up like hands, descended on the smooth, succulent flesh in a caress. The armless one used his feet as if they were hands! Seeking, probing toes skimmed caressingly over every curve of her round hips, across those tapering thighs so white in the moonlight, flickered for a moment on flat stomach only to leap suddenly higher, stroking a lush breast with a spasmodic touch.

Toes that worked, like fingers, caressing pale loveliness, warm loveliness that stirred reluctantly, squeamishly under the touch of those handlike feet.

"Clauser! Clauser!" shrieked Martin. The armless one leaped to the floor as if the sound of his name brought him

momentarily back to sanity. At the same instant the negro, Harry, sprang at him, while three muscular hands seized Martin's head and banged it on the hard floor. The moonlight faded to empty blackness.

MARTIN opened his eyes to stare directly into those of the black man. Raising his head he became aware of the unconscious girl beside him on the bed, and found that he, too, was bound, hand and foot. On the floor in the corner was the inert figure of Carl Clauser, the armless man. Dr. Lombard leaned over a table, working with instruments.

"This one's okey, chief!" Harry laughed in his face; the doctor turned quickly. Something gleamed and glittered in the lamplight.

"Aha! The demon reporter!" he sneered. "Well, my friend, you wanted an interview. You wanted to know something about my work!"

"You damned crook! You'll go to jail for this!"

"My! my!" chided the doctor. "I actually believe you thought this was a weapon! No, no, my muscular friend —this is an innocent little hypodermic needle! I'm merely going to give you a little injection of the same thing your friend Clauser had. A little medicine— an ice cream soda for the emotions!"

Martin pulled away as far as he could. The three arms of the negro wrestled with him, and he shuddered, noticing the middle one was white-skinned! Martin struggled so valiantly in spite of his bonds that Lombard was forced to aid in subduing him.

Together they held him motionless beside the still form of Helen Vinton, inserted the thin needle into the vein of his arm. Lombard spoke incessantly.

(Continued on page 111)

In the Burmese jungle lived the python demon—that slithered through the woods leaving a girl's bare footprints. And now a mysterious girl made love and vanished in the night—leaving the trail of a giant snake!

Singh lifted the speared pig. "This will get her!" he cried.

NAGA'S

THE rays of the setting sun sent long spears of light through the leafy roof of the Burmese jungle, gilding the towering trunks of teak and *pyingado*. The faint breeze wafted to Kirk Finlay's nostrils the reptilian odor of a lurking python that had evaded the native hunters.

The monster was near, but still invisible. Then a scarcely perceptible rustling almost directly overhead, and Finlay, looking up, saw the python's gaping jaws, long fangs, and incredibly thick coils.

The natives who had followed Finlay broke in panic. The American's express

KISS

By
E. HOFFMANN
PRICE

rifle snapped into line. The monster struck, lashing out like a stroke of doom as the blast of cordite shook the jungle, and Finlay knew he had missed.

The python hadn't. Its victim's agonized shriek was cut short before the python drew him into the tree. There was a hideous crunching of bones as the mon-strous coils constricted. Finlay's shoulder jerked back from the recoil of his second shot.

And as he again caught a glimpse of the python's head, Finlay fired a third shot. There was a savage, venomous hissing, and a threshing in the leaves. Something dropped from the branches, a

45

crushed, shapeless brown mass that landed at Finlay's feet with the sickening *plunk* of a saturated sponge.

"Better the *Nagâ* had eaten him, *sahib*," said a calm voice at Finlay's side. His gun bearer, Shir Singh, a giant, bearded *Sikh*, was the only one who had not fled at the first sign of the python's attack. Finlay shouted to the natives. But when he again glanced at the shapeless pulp that lay at the foot of the tree, he agreed with Shir Singh.

"Damn it," muttered Finlay, "I know I plugged it that last shot."

THE wrathful whipping in the branches had ceased. Far ahead he heard faint, even rustling. The python was making good its escape. It was unwounded and the chase was over.

Finlay, as he followed the natives back to the village, learned that he had gained a reputation.

"The great *Nagâ* fears him," was the refrain of the sing-song Burmese chatter. "She dared not touch him! She passed him to pick out another!"

Finlay began wondering. Then he reminded himself that it had likewise ignored Shir Singh; but the superstitious Burmese, already convinced that the python of Kokogon was a demon, would make something miraculous of his escape. They were jacking up their courage by ascribing to him a peculiar power over serpents.

And the local astrologer—no Burmese village is without at least a few star gazers—insisted that Finlay's horoscope proved that he was invulnerable to ophidian attack.

Which of course was pure rot. . . .

NIGHT in Burma. The long shadows of ruined pagodas marched across the compound of Finlay's *dâk* bungalow,

a hundred yards from the thorn *zariba* which enclosed the village. Buddhist monks in the adjoining monastery were intoning a ritual in Pali.

Shir Singh, after preparing and serving a pot of blistering curry, left the compound to go to the village. A *pwé* or festival was to be staged in honor of the big event: the great *Nagâ*, frightened by Finlay, had abandoned its crushed prey to take to flight. Thagya Min, King of Demons, had received a serious setback.

Finlay finally began to wonder if it would not be a good idea to join the festival. It was incredibly lonesome and eerie in the moon-haunted bungalow compound.

"Hell!" he muttered, resolving not to let native superstition get under his skin. A snake was only a snake, even though it must be at least thirty feet long. "Be damned to Thagya Min and his assorted devils."

Instead of heaping more fuel on the fire Shir Singh had kindled to dispel the chill of the Burmese night, Finlay sought the warmth of his blankets. But as he dozed, it seemed that the wind, sifting up between the cracks in the floor, was singularly penetrating.

His half sleep was troubled by the return of fancies his waking brain had expelled. A soft, stealthy rustling at last aroused him with a start. He jerked upright, reaching for his rifle.

But it was not the great *Nagâ* that had come from the forest to seek him. One of the village girls was ascending the steps of the bungalow. She wore a green skirt, slit in the Burmese fashion from ankle to hip; and her jacket of silk gauze was so thin that the moonlight made it a tenuous mist wavering about her shapely shoulders and hovering caressingly about breasts that were like lotus buds of modeled amber.

Her purple-black hair was piled high on her head, and adorned with an ivory comb. An orchid nestled in its lustrous shadow. Lovely—but just another Burmese girl.

Then Finlay noted that her oblique eyes were startlingly greenish and unwaveringly regarding him from beneath thin-penciled, high-arched brows, and in no way seconding the crimson smile which greeted Finlay as he placed her hands palm to palm and bowed the native greeting.

In spite of the mincing, pigeon-toed gait affected by the Burmese girls, the deeply slit skirt at each short step presented a glimpse of lusciously-moulded gold-bronze flesh, warm curves exposed only long enough to be an invitation and a coquetry. Each pace was a revelation withheld, and a promise about to be fulfilled. A dainty, exotic morsel, and utterly different from the women of the village.

His glance, flashing upward along the suave curve of bare hip and toward the breasts that quivered behind their silken veil, caught her eye. She had halted within arms' reach of him, and was regarding him with inscrutable, ambiguous eyes.

HE DID not rise. She was just another native girl. Finlay acknowledged her salutation, and queried, "What's the matter? Is the *pwé* getting tiresome?"

She shook her head.

"I came to ask you about the great *Nagâ*. Why are you hunting her?"

The question seemed a reproof. Finlay countered, almost defensively, "The *Nagâ* has eaten half of the village already. But what the devil—who—"

He was annoyed at having forgotten himself so far as to answer such an outrageous question.

"I'm Ma-Mya," she answered.

"That's appropriate," he admitted. "You have emerald eyes. Well, then what?"

"And the Buddha Guatama," continued the girl, "taught us to kill no living thing."

That was naive! Finlay chuckled, caught her by the hand, and observed, "He might have taken time out to teach the *Nagâ* a few things."

But Ma-Mya failed to catch the point, and perplexedly regarding him, let him draw her to his side. Though plump as a young partridge, she was a shapely armful, and the orchid in her purple-black hair enveloped Finlay in a gust of inflaming, heart-stirring fragrance that urged him to prolong the theological discussion.

"The next time I meet the great *Nagâ*," he promised, "I'll tell her she mustn't eat people."

"But she's hungry," protested the girl. "The Buddha Guatama once offered his own flesh to nourish a starving tigress."

Finlay shuddered. Buddhist legends are all right in books, but what he had witnessed that evening in the jungle made the thought seem horrible.

"Listen to them," said Ma-Mya, gesturing toward the monastery.

THE monks were at it again, chanting rituals in Pali, and beating the ringing, wooden *kaladet* in the monastery. The resonant vibration, and the reiteration of the chant sent old thrills racing through Finlay's veins.

He could not understand a word of the ancient Pali, but Ma-Mya, snuggling closer in the half gloom, whispered strange words in his ear, pleading the

Naga's case. Buddhism, Finlay quickly decided, was a mask for some older cult —the serpent worship of centuries ago.

And in spite of himself, that sibilant voice that whispered in his ear half convinced Finlay. The moon glamour, and the sonorous chanting played odd tricks with his reasoning. But Ma-Mya's slender arms and the supple curves of her closely snuggled body distracted him from his whimsical retorts to her outlandish arguments.

The amorous, golden-amber curves that peeped from the slashed skirt tempted his free hand to explore the intricacies of Burmese costume. Her smooth flesh was startlingly cold—which was not surprising—considering her fragile costume and the chill of the jungle night.

Ma-Mya shivered at Finlay's caressing touch, and her breath came in short gasps as his lips found her mouth and definitely checked the Buddhist discourse. Finlay had kissed Malay women, ivory-skinned Eurasians, Shanghai sing-song girls—but this quaint bit of loveliness from the forest of Kokogon left him dazed, shocked and fascinated.

Her red lips were as cold as her skin, yet the contact was indescribably thrilling, more sensuous than any embrace he had ever imagined; a delicious coolness to slake hottest passion. She clung to him like a chilled serpent seeking a reviving warmth; drew him to her with a silken constriction that made him wonder who was embracing, and who was embraced.

For an instant he instinctively resisted that ever tightening, possessive pressure. Then he surrendered to the uncanny fire he had kindled in that shapely girl.

There was a momentary flash of revulsion as the strange chill of her flesh bit into his very soul; but that passed.

And the Burmese night centered in that serpentine, golden brown girl. . . .

THE sunrise aroused Finlay. He was alone, and only a strand of purple black hair twined on his shoulder convinced him that Ma-Mya had not been a phantom. His lips were dry, and his brain was a whirling confusion. For a moment he thought that he had been drugged, but that tantalizing strand of hair reminded him that Ma-Mya had been no illusion.

When he stepped to the veranda, he saw fear for the first time in Shir Singh's eyes. The bearded *Sikh's* expression changed thrice in as many instants. He gestured toward the earth between the lower steps of the veranda and the entrance to the compound. It was marked by half a dozen prints of tiny, bare feet.

In the middle of the enclosure they vanished, as if blotted out. And just beyond the palisade gateway was a broad, blurred trail leading to the *zariba* that enclosed the native village: *the trace of a monstrous serpent.*

Finlay shuddered. His first thought was that Ma-Mya, leaving him as he slept, had been seized by the *Naga.* Then his horror was displaced by incredulity. Pythons lurk near the water's edge to seize unwary beasts that come to drink at sunset. Hunting in the open was a reversal of nature.

He followed the trail. As he approached the village, he heard the wailing of the natives. Moung Ba, the son of the headman, was missing.

The thorny protection of the *zariba* had been broken down. *The trail of the python vanished as abruptly as it had begun.* A woman's tiny footprints led from the breach towards the palm-thatched house of the missing Moung Ba.

Tracks in the opposite direction showed how he had followed some woman whose small, high-arched feet marked her apart from the splay footed women of the town.

had kissed him into insensibility, and sought another victim.

Finlay wiped the sudden rush of sweat from his forehead, and stretched long,

In the moon-glow he could see faint markings on her flesh.

"No python could have gone through the *zaribo*. It was a snake woman who drew the thorns aside," the Burmese insisted.

They regarded Finlay with furtive, accusing glances as they muttered. He knew now why Shir Singh had regarded him with awe; the *Sikh,* like the villagers, believed that the snake woman had lulled him to sleep so that he would not interfere with her depredations.

Since she could not attack Finlay, she

tottering legs back to the *dâk* bungalow. Such things were insane. The superstitious natives were reverting to their long abandoned serpent worship. Moung Ba had been enticed from his hut by some girl from an adjoining village. The *Nagâ* trail was pure trickery.

Then he remembered the ophidian coolness of Ma-Mya's body, and her unblinking eyes, and the subtle warmth that had drugged him as her sinuous arms encircled him with their embrace.

FINLAY seated himself on the veranda and stared at the tiny footprints that merged in the fearsome python trace. Shir Singh, seeing his sudden pallor and the deeply graved lines of his face, approached and said, "She will not come back for many days, master. She has eaten again, and she will not trouble the night."

Entering the bungalow, Finlay stared at the rumpled cot. The bedding still bore the perceptible roundness of a shapely woman's hips.

"They're crazy," he growled. But there was something odd and disturbing about the lingering sweetness of the room. He was glad that he had not seen her transformed from a woman into a serpent; as long as he had not witnessed that, his sanity would prevail.

As Shir Singh served breakfast, Sayamyo, the village headman, a stooped, wrinkled little fellow, entered the compound, paused long enough to muster up his courage, and diffidently approached Finlay, saying, "Master, the great *Nagâ* fears you, but you cannot kill her with any of your weapons. But if you go up the Chindwin River to Kalay Thoung Toht, you can there get a weapon against this monster."

"The Small Town at the Top of the Sand Bank?" echoed Finlay.

"Yes. The entire population there has supernatural power. The King of Wizards lives there. Anyone who has been bewitched can go there to plead his case. The demon will then be summoned and if there is no cause for the bewitching, he will be punished."

"Why don't you go yourself?" countered Finlay. He had to repel the insidious fancies that were eating into him.

Sayamyo shrugged, and said, "Very few people who go to Kalay Thoung Toht

ever return. But since the *Nagâ* fears you, so likewise will the King of Wizards."

"Get the hell out of here!" snapped Finlay. "I'll hunt the *Nagâ*. But I'm not messing up with native witchcraft."

That settled Sayamyo's brilliant suggestion.

Aside from their awe, the villagers were well enough disposed toward Finlay. With the disappearance of Moung Ba, it would be several weeks before the *Nagâ* came forth to seek another victim.

None of the local *shikaris* would any longer accompany Finlay on his hunts for the monstrous python; so he went with Shir Singh. But he missed Ma-Mya, and every night he lay awake, listening to the hollowly ringing *kaladets*, and wondering when that strange girl would return to translate the Pali chant, and sear his mouth with strange kisses. . . .

Every evening Finlay and Shir Singh plunged into the teak forest, seeking the *Nagâ*; but the faithful *Sikh's* grim face lengthened as he spoke of the next full moon, and the next raid of the python. The gun-bearer liked the evening hunts less and less. Finlay, however, was driven by the murmuring of the natives. He had to convince himself that she was not a serpent woman.

And then, not many days before the next full moon, when he summoned Shir Singh, there was no answer. He had deserted, rebelling against the battle with the supernatural.

"Hell with him!" grumbled Finlay, trying to laugh it off. "He's a damn' muttering pest anyhow, lately."

He picked up his rifle and headed for the jungle alone.

THE following night, Finlay awoke with a start. He recognized the strange fragrance that the evening breeze wafted into the bungalow.

Ma-Mya had returned. She was lovelier than before, and as she crossed the veranda, the deeply slashed skirt and filmy jacket revealed a delicious succession of moon-kissed curves. Not a word concerning her long absence; only her slow, crimson smile, and her sinuous arms invitingly extended.

For a moment she clung to him with a possessive fierceness that left no strength for words, then as he led her into the bungalow, she whispered things that he scarcely understood, and did not care to understand. Nothing made any difference; Ma-Mya was back again.

The uncanny closeness of her flesh, and its surprising, languorous warmth when she embraced him seemed no longer outlandish. . . .

LATER—very much later—when the moon cast a long silvery pathway into the bungalow, Ma-Mya, crossing her hands behind her head, leaned back among the pillows and whispered, "And now you won't ever hunt the great *Nagâ* any more, will you?"

The unpleasant reminder jarred Finlay. It brought back thoughts that he had been striving for several weeks to subdue.

As he regarded her slender, shapely form, stretched out in the moon glamour, rippling golden curves that smiled through the gauze that still enveloped her, he had his first real glimpse of his strange companion, and marveled anew at the fluent curves of her legs, the suave, sleek lines of her hips, and the small finely curved breasts that invited his caress.

And then he saw more, and that was disturbing—those odd, unwinking eyes, those fine white pointed teeth, and the ripple that seemed to undulate along her outstretched body as she shifted herself among the pillows.

In the white moonglow, he now saw that her thighs, stomach, and breasts were faintly mottled with diamond-shaped markings, like the shadow pattern in a Hamadan rug.

Her skin had a strange and alluring iridescence as she stirred and breathed. Python markings—the lustre of serpent skin!

Horror for a moment blended with desire. Finlay had to prove to himself once for all that this girl was not woman and serpent in one.

"Certainly, I'm going to hunt the *Nagâ*," he harshly declared, thrusting her away from him. The contact sent a tingling through his blood. Her arms followed up her advantage and drew him to her hungry lips.

He felt the sensuous ripple of her body, felt the chill of her flesh become a languorous warmth, and it no longer made any difference whether she was woman or serpent. . . .

FINLAY'S awakening was as before: dizzy, half-drugged and uncertain on his feet. The outcries of the Burmese villagers told him what had happened during the night. He stalked towards the *zariba*. The thorns had again been cast aside. A serpent trail led to the breach in the barrier.

Leading from it were the tiny footprints of a woman and the larger prints of her victim, heading towards the fringe of the jungle.

Finlay prepared his own breakfast. And all day he sat on the veranda, hunched forward and smoking one cigarette after another.

"It's coincidence . . . those markings on her body don't mean anything," he reiterated, struggling to salvage what remained of his sanity; but the effort was thankless, and his final decision was only an expression of defeat.

"I'll go to Kalay Thoung Toht," he declared. "I'll see the King of Wizards, and find out once and for all."

But Finlay decided to go once more into the teak forest to hunt the *Naga*. After swallowing its victim, it would be in a lethargy, and would be easy to kill. This induced Sayamyo, the headman, to furnish *shikaris*.

Finlay knew that at the first sight of the mighty serpent, his allies would turn tail and run. But that made no difference. He would face that demon snake rather than consult a native wizard.

That evening, shortly before sunset Finlay set out across the clearing, followed by half of the village. His gun was loaded with explosive bullets. A single well placed shot would once for all dissipate the hideous fear that had crept into his brain.

And that done, he could look forward to Ma-Mya's return, and enjoy her strange loveliness without a lingering qualm. He gestured to silence the singsong chatter, and the beating of drums and gongs, and the shooting of firecrackers which the Burmese *shikaris* were using to fortify their own courage.

"Shut up, you damn' fools! Even if a snake can't hear, there's no sense in that."

They were now skirting the reedy bank of the *jeel* where the *Naga* had formerly seized her victims; but Finlay swung left and into the forest, where he hoped to find the gorged monster.

"Not that way, master," cautioned the headman as Finlay picked up a barely perceptible trail. "That is the path to Kalay Thoung Toht."

The road to the village of wizards. He circled for a moment. Then picked up the footprints of the missing man and his mysterious temptress. To find them would clarify the riddle, and clear Ma-Mya.

"This way!" shouted Finlay, gesturing up the trail. He bounded forward. His courage was contagious. The villagers followed; but only until they learned that they were trailing human footprints, and those of one who should have no feet. They halted. There was a sombre muttering—but it was interrupted.

A FLAT, elongated head the size of a small nail keg suddenly darted from overhead, scarcely disturbing the foliage as it swayed slowly right and left, its glittering elliptical eyes appraising its enemy. The leaves parted, and several yards of the monster's body reached out and downward.

It was thicker than a man's thigh, and the coils half visible in the slanting light were even larger where it was wrapped around the branches. Finlay snapped his rifle to his shoulder. As his eyes flashed along the sights, he wondered why the natives had not broken and fled.

"She has not eaten!" they cried. "She is thin and hungry—this is not the demon *Naga*."

But it was the great *Naga*. It was yellowish brown in color, with diamond shaped bluish-black markings ridged with white. A thin black line extended from the end of the snout down to the nape of the neck. No two pythons have the identical markings, and Finlay, as he aligned the sights of his rifle, was certain that this was his prey.

That it was not lethargic from having swallowed the last of the uncannily vanished victims made his heart hammer violently. That proved that Ma-Mya was not a snake woman.

It was a fearsome creature that faced
Finlay, fully thirty feet of iron muscle,
tense and vibrant, ready to swoop down
and select a victim. In the slanting sunlight the iridescent colors mirrored in its
countless scales made it a thing of terrible beauty. No wonder that they called
it a demon.

Finlay's trigger finger contracted. The
nitrous blast of cordite ripped the jun-

The great coils grew nebulous . . .
No longer did he feel the pressure
of the snake.

gle's silence. A crashing report followed.
The explosive bullet, instead of tearing
through the frontal plates of the python's
armor, had buried itself into the tree
trunk and exploded.

FINLAY realigned the barrel. His
elation at knowing that Ma-Mya was
not a serpent had made him miss an easy
shot; and the swaying menacing head of
the monster was not an easy target. He
fired again.

The sights were directly in line between the elliptical unwinking eyes. But
swiftly as Finlay pressed the trigger, he
was an instant too late. It seemed that

the monster's incredible velocity had out-stripped the blast of smokeless powder.

Even as with the instinct of a trained marksman, Finlay "spotted" his shot, a terrific, crushing impact struck the rifle from his shoulder. A loop of tawny golden brown encircled him like a lariat. The python's neck, arching like a horse-shoe, bent down as if to inspect the prey that was now enveloped from shoulder to ankles in loop after loop of murderous contriction.

The great jaws, gleaming with long, sharp ivory white teeth, gaped open, wide enough to swallow an antelope.

His breath was cut off by the inexorable pressure of that gigantic coil; he felt no pain, for the vise-like pressure had numbed him beyond sensation. There was a drumming in his ears, and red motes flashed before his eyes as he vainly struggled, clawing and beating against the scaly armor of the great *Nagâ*.

As from a great distance he heard the shrieking of the natives: "His magic is broken. The great *Nagâ* does not fear him. We are lost."

A crackling and rustling in the under-brush, and the voices dimmed in the distance. The ruddy sunset glow was becoming an impenetrable blackness, shot with long streaks of electric blue and lurid blazing red.

Finlay's sense of touch was likewise gone, and he but dimly felt the licking tongue that lashed over his face. He seemed to be falling, dropping into bottomless space. The chill of horror no longer racked him. A pleasant, languorous warmth gradually suffused through his numbed limbs. It seemed that he no longer needed to breathe. And the chill of that monstrous embrace began to feel strangely familiar . . . like Ma-Mya's possessive arms. . . .

THEN he sensed that his feet were on the ground. The crushing pressure no longer made his ribs crack. He inhaled a long, shuddering breath. The gloom receded and became a misty bluish grayness through which long red lances of sunlight filtered. The great coils had become nebulous. Finlay saw that the serpent was gone. Only its reptilian exhalation lingered in the quiet evening air; something cool and moist still caressed his cheek.

Then his eyes drew into focus. Ma-Mya's arms supported him. He shuddered as he realized that she had materialized out of the space occupied by the serpent!

"Don't be afraid," she murmured in that familiar, sibilant whisper. "I have power over serpents, and I frightened the great *Nagâ* away. Your power failed, and she attacked you. But let's go away from that village. They try to kill her instead of winning her over by kindness."

Ma-Mya caught him by the hand and advanced into the deeper gloom of the forest. Finlay followed, glad to accept her explanation. But he was shaken and trembling, and when he tripped over a root, he collapsed in a heap. Ma-Mya seated herself on the ground beside him, to wait for his recovery.

"Now you see why I wanted you not to hunt the great *Nagâ*," she whispered in his ear. "I knew sooner or later she would get over her fear of you—"

Finlay was no longer certain of anything. The odd discoloration of Ma-Mya's skin and the iridescence of her flesh made a simmering madness of his brain. She sensed the conviction that he no longer could repel. She smiled sadly and said, "I'm one of the serpent people —I didn't want you to know. But I had to frighten them away. Don't be afraid of me. I'll love you as no human woman ever could. . . ."

Finlay welcomed madness. He believed her, and the truth no longer horrified him. He gathered her in his arms, and sought her thirsty lips, knowing now that he sought a *Nagâ's* kisses. . . .

Behind them was a sudden crackling, and a stealthy rustling. Ma-Mya, startled, broke from his arms and glanced sharply to her left. Her body became tense, and her expression changed. Her eyes gleamed with fear and wrath, and Finlay, struggling to his knees, whirled about.

A MAN, turning from the trail where Finlay had dropped his rifle, was approaching them. Shir Singh, haggard and tattered, his beard disheveled and streaming. In his hands he carried a short lance on the point of which was transfixed a young pig.

Its bristles had been shaved off, and the skin was marked with designs in blue and red: curious figures such as Finlay had seen sculptured in the ruined temples of Pâgan.

Shir Singh was trembling, but his eyes glowed like coals in the darkness. The fellow was stark mad, and about to wreak his superstitious wrath on Ma-Mya.

"Drop it, you damn' fool!" shouted Finlay. But the *Sikh* did not hear him. He was staring at a wonder utterly beyond comprehension. Finlay turned, and also saw.

Ma-Mya's body was becoming translucent, shrouded in gathering that seemed to emerge from the sombre, ever-thickening shadows. It was as though hundreds of ghostly serpents were blending with her body to form a single monstrous *Nagâ*. The phantom serpent's tail whipped about the trunk of a tree.

It became more substantial, until in the dying evening glow there was the duplicate of the python which had seized Finlay.

Finlay could neither shout nor move. The *Sikh* stood petrified. Time had ceased.

Then it happened. A horrible hissing, and the monster lashed out, looping about the *Sikh*. But lightning swift as it was, Shir Singh was equally fast. One powerful arm was free. He rammed the lance and its grotesque burden squarely into the gaping jaws of the *Nagâ*.

A strangled yell. The constricting terror was closing around the stalwart giant. Finlay tried to look away but could not. The *Sikh* was doomed, but his weapon took effect. There was a frantic threshing. The *Nagâ* uncoiled. Fumes and flame gushed from the gaping jaws.

Then a terrific blast, a surge of fire, but horror blotted Finlay's senses before he could see the end.

When he opened his eyes, a single shaft of moonlight filtered through the leafy roof of the jungle. There was a stirring near him. He clambered to his feet. In the gloom he recognized Shir Singh, crushed but still alive. There was something else near the *Sikh,* something which Finlay did not want to see, but which he could not avoid examining.

It was what was left of a woman's body. A hideous tangle of flesh and bone. Enough remained intact for him to recognize Ma-Mya. The weapon which had destroyed the great *Nagâ* had blasted asunder that lovely girl who had sought him by moonlight. . . .

Finlay bounced to the path. He snatched his rifle from the ground, snapped a cartridge into the chamber. He leaped back again, halting a few paces from the *Sikh*.

(Continued on page 120)

Beautiful, feminine legs—but they were disembodied spectres of a dead girl—seeking her body! Did the secret lie with the Doctor of Death or with the shrunken mummified heads of Astro?

DEAD

L IVID-WHITE and weirdly-glowing, the legs gleamed against solid darkness in Dexter's bedroom. A woman's legs, beautiful, naked, tapering into exquisitely-turned ankles, swelling upward toward perfect feminine thighs. And above the thighs—*nothingness!*

Cold globules of horror-sweat suddenly collected on Dexter's brow. He sat upright in the bed, staring. The room was pitch dark, as though the night had

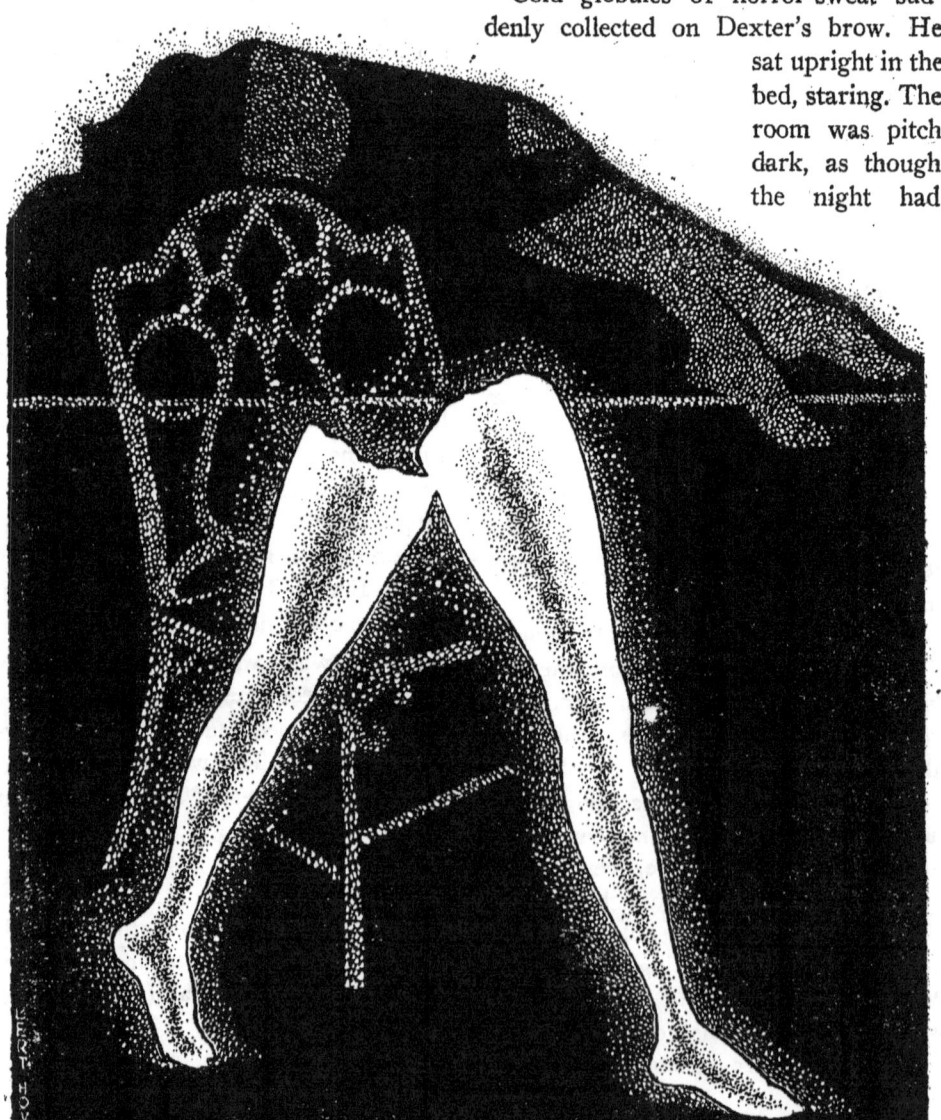

LEGS WALK

stifled all illumination with a sinister, blanketing shroud. And against the blackness, those bloodless, phosphorescent *legs*. . . .

They were moving; they were coming toward Dexter, slowly, implacably.

Thralls of terror held him gyved, helpless. He could not move; could not breathe. What monstrous, malefic evil was this that sank its fangs into his soul? The disembodied legs were coming closer. . . closer. . . .

**By
JEROME
SEVERS
PERRY**

Ghostly, lovely, they were walking towards him!

Suddenly, before his distended eyes, the gleaming legs vanished. Disappeared. Were swallowed up in the engulfing folds of darkness.

Dexter's dilated pupils ached with the savage strain of staring into the utter blackness that surrounded him. Moments passed; moments filled with unutterable fear. Then, slowly, he broke through the fettering chrysails of terror that had bound him. He staggered to his feet, fumbled for the light-button, pressed it.

THE room's shaded lamps glowed into life. Dexter swept the chamber with his gaze. Abruptly, a cold chill brushed his flesh. "My God!" he gasped.

He stared at two white objects by his bed. Two legs, amputated well above the knees; blood-drained, ghastly-white, perfectly-formed. The disembodied legs that Dexter had seen walking toward him. . . . !

Then it hadn't been a nightmare. He hadn't dreamed that he had seen the legs moving of their own volition. It had been real—horribly real! The spine-jellying actuality of it was evidenced by the amputated legs themselves. They lay on the floor at his feet. And when, gingerly, he touched them, he felt the smoothness of cold, dead flesh. . . .

And what was that?

There was an envelope on the carpet, sealed with a crimson splash of wax that seemed somehow like a drop of congealed blood. There was a harsh curse at the back of Dexter's constricted throat as he leaned forward and picked up the sealed rectangle of paper. He stared at it blankly.

It was addressed in blood-red ink: "Mr. Pat Dexter, publisher, *Daily Clarion*. Personal and Important!" The writing had been done with a thick, heavy pen; the characters were formed with a weird, shapeless irregularity, almost like sinister hieroglyphs of horror.

Dexter ripped the envelope open, extracted a single sheet of note-paper that crackled like ancient parchment under his fingers. And as he read, his eyes widened. "Damn them! Damn them to hell!" he rasped.

Again he read the note—

"Dexter:

This is what happens to meddlers. Not just death alone; but mutilation as well. Mutilation and soul-destruction. Legs that must walk, undead, through the night; that must walk in horrible search for the bodies of which they were once a part. Searching in vain for the bodies that have been destroyed. . .

Take heed. You have already gone too far in your campaign of vilification. The next time, it may be the lovely legs of your fiancee, Doris Killian—the girl you adore.

The Doctor of Death."

A strangled, choking sound issued from Dexter's dry, rasping throat. The thing was monstrous—fantastic—impossible! It couldn't be true. And yet. . . there were those two dead legs on his floor, mute and grisly evidence of what he had seen with his own eyes in the darkness.

Sudden frenetic rage burned in Dexter's brain, and his eyes became narrowed slits in his rugged face. Either he had gone mad, or else he had stumbled into a miasmatic maelstrom of hellish, fiendish foulness. And he knew that he was not mad. . . .

He leaped for his closet, flung himself into his clothes. That evil, red-inked note had threatened Doris Killian

—the girl he loved with all his soul. Perhaps she had already fallen into the clutches of the demoniac fiend who had penned those sinister words. . . .

Dexter hurled himself out of the house, raced for his car in the garage at the rear. Some malignant fate seemed to hover over him this night, for he found one of his tires deflated, flat. It took him five soul-wrenching minutes to change it.

Then he slid behind the wheel, slammed into gear and headed desperately toward the house where Doris Killian lived with her half-sister, Edith, and Edith's husband, Tom Sloane.

THE Sloane house was on the outskirts of town. Dexter braked his coupe to a skidding, tire-consuming halt before the unlighted bungalow and leaped for the front door. Savagely he pounded on the closed portal.

After a long moment, a light showed; the door opened. Tom Sloane, grey-haired and drowsy and clad in pajamas, stared at Dexter. "Hello, Pat. What's wrong? You look excited."

"Where is Doris? Is she here? Is she . . . safe?"

"Why, of course she's here. She's in bed. It's after midnight, you know." Tom Sloane's eyes looked curiously into Dexter's. "You're acting funny, Pat. What's on your mind?"

Dexter brushed past him, into the house. "I want to see Doris!"

A bedroom door opened at the rear of the short corridor; a girl stepped into the hallway. She was young, red-haired, insouciantly lovely.

She was clad in a sheer, clinging nightgown of thin silk, through which her boyish hips and small, pointed breasts were silhouetted with delicious candor. She saw Dexter, and her hazel eyes widened. "Pat!" she exclaimed in surprise, as she took a hesitant step forward.

Dexter sprang toward her, grabbed her in his arms. Her slim, virginal young body melted against him thrillingly, and he could feel the boyish firmness of her tiny breasts thrusting against his chest. "Doris!" he whispered. "You—you're all right? There's nothing wrong with you? Nothing has. . . happened to you?"

She smiled at him, sleepily, bewilderdly. "Nothing wrong with me? Of course not! What on earth—"

From another room, a second girl suddenly appeared. It was Doris Killian's older sister, Edith. She, too, was clad only in a revealing nightgown; her heavy breasts, her voluptuous curves, were the mature fulfillment of the feminine promise in the slenderness of her sister. Edith Sloane's red lips opened in a startled smile. "What's going on here, anyhow?" she demanded lightly.

Pat Dexter frowned. "There's something mysterious and sinister taking place in this town. And a threat has been made against Doris."

"A threat?" Tom Sloane started.

"Yes. It develops that I have an enemy—one who calls himself Doctor of Death. And he threatens to strike at me through Doris; threatens to kill her —and worse—"

"What do you mean, worse?" Doris Killian's slim form tensed against Dexter's body.

DEXTER'S eyes narrowed. "It's too fantastic to be believable, my sweet. And yet—I've seen it with my own eyes. Disembodied legs that walk through the night, gleaming and phosphorescent and weird. Legs that walk in the midnight, seeking the body from which they were torn!" His voice held a shudder-timbre of horror.

Tom Sloane stared; then, slowly, he grinned. "I never knew that you went in for practical joking, Pat. What's come over you, anyhow?"

"It's not a joke!" Dexter snapped harshly. "I tell you, *I have seen dead legs walking!* And now those legs are lying on the floor of my bedroom—bloodless, lifeless, horrible!" There was such cold horror in his voice that all three of his listeners went slowly pale. They stared at him.

Then Tom Sloane spoke. "But who would—would do a thing like that? Who *could* do a thing like that? It's unearthly—it isn't possible! You must have had a bad dream, Pat!"

"It was no dream. And I think I know who is responsible. Lately I have been conducting an editorial campaign in my paper, trying to run the charlatan fortune-tellers and astrologers and crystal-gazers out of this town. They're blood-suckers, every one of them; bleeding money out of ignorant, superstitious dupes who have no better sense than to patronize them.

"In particular, I've thundered against a certain Professor Astro, who moved into the old Yancey house a few weeks ago. He's the worst of the lot, and I've been singling him out for my attacks in the editorial columns of the *Clarion*. It's my guess that this is his way of trying to shut me up!"

Doris Killian shuddered in Dexter's enfolding arms. "And he—he has threatened me?" she whispered fearfully.

"Yes!" Dexter's brow was furrowed with deep lines of impotent worry. "But I can't prove anything against him. I have no evidence!"

Tom Sloane laughed uneasily. "In any case, he can't possibly do any harm to Doris. How could he get to her, here in this house?"

Then Sloane's wife, Edith, came forward nervously. "I wonder" she whispered fearfully.

"What?" Dexter barked.

"Cecile, our maid, has been gone since last night. She's disappeared. You—you don't suppose she could have fallen into the hands of this Professor Astro—?"

ABRUPTLY, Dexter remembered those dead, amputated legs in the bedroom of his own house. A sudden tightness leaped into his throat. He sprang toward the telephone at the other end of the hallway, unpronged the receiver, rattled the hook savagely.

"Hello—get me the police department —quick!" he barked. Then, after a momentary silence, "Police headquarters? This is Pat Dexter, publisher of the *Clarion*. I want you to send a detective to my house right away. I'll meet him in five minutes." He slammed up the receiver, turned to the others.

"Listen, Tom Sloane. You too, Edith. I want you to guard Doris tonight—watch over her. I have a queer presentiment of evil. Call it a hunch if you like. But I want you to guard her."

Tom Sloane's lips parted in a worried effort to smile. "Of course we will, Pat. We'll take care of her. And as administrator of Doris' estate, I stand ready to spend any amount of money to insure her safety. You know that."

Dexter grunted. He grabbed at Doris Killian's lovely form, pulled her to him, planted a hungry kiss on her moist red lips. For a single instant he felt the electrifying tip of her darting tongue; his hands pressed upon her little breasts through the thin silk of her nightgown.

Then he turned and hurled himself out of the house.

A plain-clothes man from headquarters was already waiting outside Dexter's residence when he got there, a few hurried minutes later. Dexter caught the detective's arm, drew him toward the

He threw himself on the figure, tore it away from the girl's throat.

front door. "In some mysterious fashion, a woman's amputated legs got into my bedroom a while ago!" he rasped.

"1 want you to carry them down to the morgue—and then institute a search for the corpse from which they were disjointed. I have an idea that this is a murder case!"

The detective drew a sharp breath. Together, the two men entered Dexter's house; went into his bedroom.

Dexter snapped on the lights. "Right there—" he started to point. And then a crepitant chill swept down his spine, and his flesh crawled horribly over his congealing bones. *The bloodless, amputated feminine legs had vanished!*

The detective looked oddly at Pat Dexter. "You're sure you weren't seein' things, sir?"

Dexter flushed. "I wish to God I had been!" he rasped. "Those amputated legs were here, a few minutes ago. A woman's legs. I saw them with my own eyes!"

"Maybe they walked away," the detective suggested facetiously.

Dexter shuddered; and it seemed as though icy fingers were dipping into his brain. "God help me, I think that's what they did!" he whispered. Then he glared at the detective. "I know. You think I've gone insane. Well, help yourself. Go ahead and think what you damned please! But no matter what you think, I know—because *I saw!*" The words on his tongue were thick with a nameless dread.

THE detective shrugged. And a little later, after a fruitless search for the missing legs, he departed. Dexter was alone, and his mind was full of a hammering kaleidoscope of gibbering fancies. The silence of the house pressed sardonically upon his consciousness; a slithery voice seemed to be whispering of unnamed evils and malignant, horrific impossibilities. . . .

Abruptly, Dexter squared his broad, athletic shoulders. Professor Astro was behind this weird night's work; Professor Astro, crystal-gazer and fake daemonologist! "I'll face him! I'll crush the truth out of him with my naked hands!" Dexter gritted. He leaped for the front door, flung himself out into the black night.

It took him ten minutes of insane, reckless driving to reach the old Yancey house, on the edge of the city.

The place was a brooding, rococo frame structure overshadowed by ancient, gnarled trees that whispered with a thousand sinister tongues in the night wind. Grotesque wooden ornamentation, twisted carvings, rotting and weather-decayed filigrees marked every inch of the black facade of the house; shuttered, unlighted windows loomed like closed eyes of a corpse.

Over house and unkempt, weed-grown grounds there seemed to hover a queer, dank odor of dampness and dissolution and . . . death. . . .

Dexter shuddered as he lunged out of his coupe and approached the evil-omened structure. So this was where Professor Astro had his headquarters! The place, in the darkness, was even worse than Dexter had pictured it by daylight. A malevolent, noxious atmosphere of foreboding permeated the very air that surrounded the house. In the trees above Dexter's head, a bat flitted eerily. . . . An owl hooted. . . .

Dexter reached the sagging front porch. Rain-rotted boards creaked and gave under his heels; his weight sank into spongy, decayed wood with a weird sensation, as though he trod upon putrefied flesh. . . .

He saw an ancient brass knocker on the door, cast in the form of a grinning human skull, green with verdigris and slimy with dew-moisture. He stifled a shudder of revulsion as he extended his hand toward the repugnant, grinning skull—

The door swung open in his face, groaning on protesting hinges. Dexter stared into the slanted, oddly-gleaming eyes of a man who was smiling at him with a thin-lipped, cat-like smile.

"I am Professor Astro. And you are Pat Dexter, owner of the *Clarion*. Why do you seek me at this late hour, Mr. Dexter?"

Dexter stiffened. For the first time, he noticed the queer, repellent slant of Astro's dark eyebrows; the peaked point of black hair on the man's forehead; the black wisp of goatee that added a Satanic look to the man's sharp, sallow features. And Astro's voice had been purring, slurred, feline. . . .

"How did you know my name? How did you know I was here?" Dexter demanded raspingly.

"Astro knows all things. Come in, Mr. Dexter. You will perhaps be more . . . er, comfortable, inside."

DEXTER hesitated. Then his jaw shot forward pugnaciously. "Thank you!" he snapped sarcastically. He followed the crystal-gazer into the gloomy, hollowly-resounding depths of the musty house.

They entered a shuttered room. There was a single lamp flickering in one corner, blue-shaded and eerie. It cast a ghoulish illumination upon the shadowy corners, and in the blue light Astro's features took on a sinister corpse-pallor, like long-dead flesh. . . .

Dexter stared about him. Piled on shelves he saw ancient, queerly-lettered parchment manuscripts, yellow with age. There were paintings upon the walls— horrible, loathsome, revulsion-stirring

painting that almost seemed to move and grimace as Dexter glanced at them.

A blasphemous nightmare-carving crouched in one dim corner, furry, foul, diabolic. On a table in the center of the room, Dexter saw three tiny heads fastened to an oblong onyx plate. His eyes widened. Those heads were . . . human! They were the shriveled, mummified heads of infants. . . .

Professor Astro smiled gently. "You are interested in my Teraphim, Mr. Dexter? They are very ancient. Once they were the household gods of a Semite priest, in the days before Solomon. To the one who understands the secret of unlocking their tongues, they can tell many strange things!"

Dexter drew a sharp breath. In spite of himself, he cast another sidelong glance at those three wrinkled, mummified heads which Astro had called Teraphim. Then he forced his gaze to meet Astro's cat-like, green-glowing eyes. "Enough of this nonsense!" he barked savagely. "You know damned well you can't scare me with your magic hocus-pocus! And you know what I'm here for!"

Astro shrugged. "You are probably here to advise me to leave the city. You think, perhaps, that your own personal threats will sway me more than your pettifogging editorials have done. Well, you are wrong, my friend. Here I am, and here I stay. And may I speak just a word of friendly warning? It does not pay to meddle too much in the affairs of Professor Astro. Others have found that out—to their eternal sorrow!" His voice held a hissing, sinuous quality, as though a snake had given tongue to the words.

Dexter sneered. "Your threats leave me cold, Astro. And meanwhile I want you to know that I realize you sent me that red-written letter. I know that you were behind the affair of those disembodied legs that walked of their own volition. And now—*what have you done with the corpse of Cecile, Tom Sloane's French maid?*"

Astro's eyes narrowed. "You speak in riddles, my friend."

ABRUPTLY, Dexter plunged his hand into the pocket of his coat. He withdrew a flat, snub-nosed automatic, leveled it at the crystal-gazer's midriff. "I'm going to search your house, Astro. And you're going with me!" he snarled.

Astro bowed, veiling the gleam that leaped into his cat-like eyes. "I defer to your commands, Mr. Dexter," he purred. "Where would you prefer to look first?"

"We'll start here on the lower floor. What's that next room?" Dexter gestured toward a closed door.

Astro paled. "That room is private. You shall not enter it!"

"No? We'll see about that!" Dexter's finger tightened about the automatic's trigger. *"Open that door!"*

Astro's eyes licked the room as though seeking escape. Then, very slowly, he turned and went to the closed door which Dexter had indicated. He rasped a key into the ancient lock, turned it. The door swung open.

The faint blue effulgence of the weird lamp's rays penetrated into the room through the opened portal. A fetid odor poured out of the chamber, like a noxious wave. Astro suddenly swayed. "Oh, my God!" he cried out harshly.

Dexter leaped forward, staring. There on the floor at his feet lay something white, still, gruesome—

It was the naked, dead corpse of Tom Sloane's missing maid—*and her legs had been crudely amputated above the knees!*

Dexter's throat tightened. His eyes widened in horror at the sight of that mutilated feminine corpse. The dead girl's eyes were open, staring up into nothingness. Her nude body gleamed weirdly in the bluish light; her breasts, firm and heavy and crimson-centered were rounded melons of pathetic, lifeless beauty.

And her swelling white thighs ended horribly in blood-raw, hacked ends of flesh from which pinkish bones protruded nauseatingly. . . .

Astro sagged toward Dexter. "You—you killer!" he cried out wildly. "You did this! You planted her in here, so you'd have something on me! So you could force me to leave town—!"

Dexter's lips drew back in a snarling, grim smile. "It won't work, Astro. You can't fool me. You killed this girl as a threat to me. And you'll hang for it!"

There was a heavy, blood-crimson drape hanging on the near wall. Dexter seized its tasseled velvet cord, yanked it down with a savage pull. Then, swiftly, efficiently, he trussed the crystal-gazer by wrists and ankles, dumped his roped form on the floor. "Now I'm going to phone the police!" he snarled.

HE raced through the ancient, sinister house. But there was no telephone. Cursing, Dexter launched himself out into the black night, leaped into his car, headed it toward town.

He found an all-night lunch-room, jammed himself into a phonebooth, dialed police headquarters. "This is Dexter of the *Clarion* again!" he barked hurriedly. "I've located the body of the murdered woman whose legs disappeared from my house a while ago. And—I've got your murderer for you! Got him tied up! It's Professor Astro, that fake

"You murdered her," shouted Dexter. "You'll hang for it!"

mystic who's been operating in the old Yancey place. I've tied him up in his own house. Send your men there at once!"

Dexter hung up and raced back to his parked coupe. As he neared Astro's dark and foreboding house, he heard the weird wailing song of police sirens behind him. A touring car loaded with uniformed men drew up behind him as he entered the grounds of the sinister house.

Dexter placed himself at the head of the squad of headquarters men. Leaped up to the rotting porch. Smashed open the front door and sped into the mildewed, noisome interior. An evil silence seemed to brood over the house; *and the blue light had disappeared!*

In the flickering, dancing white rays of police flashlights, Dexter found the room in which he had left Astro trussed up; in which he had found the murdered girl's mutilated corpse. With the police at his heels, he launched himself into the room. And then his breath went out in a whistling, gasping exhalation.

Astro had vanished! And the corpse was not there!

There followed a swift, thorough search of the dark, foul-smelling house— from cellar to garret. But there was no trace of Professor Astro; no trace of the dead girl's nude body.

Abruptly, a crawling sensation of evil assailed Dexter's senses. The fake mystic had escaped. And now, in revenge, he might be planning some horrific vengeance; might already be on his way to the Sloane house, where Doris Killian lived . . .Dexter tensed. . . .

Before the police could stay him, before they could question him, he dived out through the front door; found his parked coupe; slammed himself behind the wheel; rocketed the machine forward through the darkness of the city's deserted streets.

Each crawling second, each flashing intersection past which he sped, seemed like an eternity to Pat Dexter. His knuckles were white as he gripped the steeringwheel. His knee trembled with the pressure of his foot on the throttle. His motor roared a thrumming challenge to the night as the coupe hurtled onward. The wind whistled eerily, demonically, around his windshield—

At last he skidded to a stop before Tom Sloane's house, flung himself to the front door, pounded on its savagely. The door opened. Tom Sloane stared at him.

"Listen!" Dexter rasped. "I found the body of your maid, Cecile, in Astro's house. I captured Astro—but he escaped before the police could get there. Now Astro's at large. . . and Doris is in danger! I'm going to take her to my place. She'll be safe with me!" he patted the flat weight of the automatic in his coat pocket.

DORIS KILLIAN'S bedroom door opened The slender, virginal redhaired girl stepped out into the hallway. Dexter ran toward her, grabbed her in his arms. Before she could protest, he had lifted her; carried her out to his waiting coupe. Clad only in her sheer nightgown, she trembled against him as he drove with grim haste toward his own home.

At last he reached his goal. With Doris Killian by his side, Pat Dexter entered the house. "I'm going to put you to bed in my room. And I'm going to stand guard over you, the rest of the night!" he whispered.

Doris blushed deliciously. "But—Pat, darling, that's a little unconventional—"

"To the devil with conventions!

There's something fiendish, clammy, foul, going on tonight. And I'm going to be at your side every minute!" He guided her into his bedroom; watched her as she snuggled like a tired kitten under the covers.

In the pink-shaded glow of a lamp near the bed, Doris Killian was an enticing picture. Her auburn hair streamed down over delicately-curved shoulders, and her features were wistfully beautiful. Through the thin, sheer silk of her gown, Dexter could see the faint pink circles, up-thrust and nubile, that marked the centers of her firm little breasts. . . . She smiled at him.

"Don't you think you've overestimated the powers of this Professor Astro, Pat?" she whispered. "Surely he wouldn't dare—"

"He dared to kill Cecile, your sister's maid. That was to warn me. That was to lend weight to the threat he made against you. And now that I've uncovered him as a murderer, he's likely to go to any lengths for revenge!" Dexter answered harshly.

Doris shivered. "You make me feel afraid," she whispered.

"You needn't be afraid. Nothing will happen to you now!" Pat Dexter sat on the edge of the bed, caught the trembling girl in his hard arms, enfolded her in his protecting embrace. She clung to him; and he could feel the beating of her heart against his chest.

"Beloved!" he whispered. . . . He kissed her. . . .

Her red lips parted, opened under the questing, seeking pressure of his mouth. Little darts of desire danced down his spine, thrillingly. His fingers drew the shoulder-straps of her sheer nightgrown down over her arms, unveiling the unmatured loveliness of her small, boyish breasts.

Gently, his palms enclosed those rounded, firm little mounds; caressed them. . . . His lips wandered over her eyes, her cheeks, downward to the warmly-scented hollow of her white throat. . . .

She pressed herself against him, trembling on the verge of surrender. Capitulation glowed in her slumbrous eyes. Through the thin silk of her nightgown, he felt the slender curves of her hips, the firm sweetness of her thighs. . .

Her arms were locked about his neck, drawing him toward her gently, ardently. . . . Her lithe, vibrant body clung to him as he pressed her close. . . .

WHAT was that?

The pink-shaded lamp had flickered. Now, abruptly it winked out. The room was plunged into absolute, utter darkness!

Pat Dexter tried to leap to his feet. But the white, clinging arms of Doris Killian were about him, terrified, locking him to her with chains of crawling fear. And then, suddenly, against the solid blackness of the room, something glowed with a weird, hellish luminosity—

Legs!

Feminine, disjointed, disembodied legs, livid-white and gleaming with a ghastly, grisly phosphorescence! Beautiful, naked legs, ghost-glowing and perfect in their macabre beauty! Legs that tapered into exquisitely-turned ankles; that swelled upward toward livid, modeled thighs. And above the thighs— *nothingness!*

"Oh, God! Oh, my God! Pat—save me! Don't let them—!" Doris Killian's voice was a clammy moan in her flawless throat. She clung to Dexter, her body racked with convulsive shudders of terror.

(Continued on page 124)

HELL HOLE

Was she a wraith, this mystery girl of the Black Forest? What evil spell linked her with the crawling Terror . . . bound her to the woman who was Mistress of the Monsters?

THE dense clear-green foliage of giant firs, rising in pyramided whorls fifty feet above the matted floor of the forest, obscured the mauve blanket of twilight sky, as Lane Wilbur beat his way through the tangled undergrowth, a flop-eared hound lopping at his side.

Now he was the cool, calm woodsman, at home with the towering trees and the clean, pungent smell of the forest. And yet, only hours before, as he stalked from Chief Willoughby's office, his blood had boiled in his veins like the oily brew in a witch's cauldron.

The police official's last words rang in Lane's ears as his keen, gray eyes searched the ground for the jagged, pithy ends of cracked twigs, or any other sign of human passing.

"Don't meddle with it, Lane," Willoughby had said. "We've been two weeks on the case and we're up against a stone wall."

Lane had flared up. "And that's your answer to the kidnaping of an infant

As he beat at the mask of a face before him, he heard the girl's horrified voice.

By
DON KING

of HORROR

from its crib? You're up against a stone wall? You're through, is that it?"

The worry lines on Willoughby's parchment face deepened. "I hate to say it, Lane, but it's true." His voice was tired and empty. "It's not the first Elkins baby to go like that. There's a

curse on **Colonel Matt Elkins' family,** a curse that's no part of anything human.

"The day Colonel Matt retired from the circus business, his second born was kidnaped. Roy Elkins was nine or ten at the time. Now it's his baby. In between there were five others . . . . all branches of the family." He shook his gray head. "It's not human, Lane."

Hot anger had foamed at Lane's lips. "Why don't you call in outside help if you can't handle it?" he demanded. "How long does this go on, human or not?"

"You've been away too long, Lane," Willoughby replied quietly. "We did all that. Got the best bloodhound pack in the State, and a detective from the city. The dogs traced the scent to the Black Forest. They went in and the detective followed them. We found dogs and man the next morning . . . . dead! *Dead from rattlesnake bites!"*

AND now Lane was breaking a trail through the Black Forest, searching for a spoor that two weeks of continual rain had probably obliterated. However, the intensity with which he despised the attitude of the *Little River* dwellers in regard to the kidnaping of Roy Elkins' six-months'-old babe, lent impetus to the almost blind trek into the forest gloom.

A break in the lofty tree-tops showed a patch of leaden sky splashed with the orange rays of the setting sun. The ground-gloom was deepening. It was time to turn back. Night in the Black Forest was an ebony pitch.

The sharp edge of a steel hatchet, which he had used to blaze the trail from the forest's edge, bit into the trunk of a thick fir, cutting the bark away in an inverted V. That would serve to indicate where the trail was to be taken up again in the morning.

Lane called to the hound who had vaulted a rotting tree trunk and was sniffing its ant-infested decay. On the heels of his voice he heard a hollow, ominous rattle. There was no mistaking the sound. It was a diamond-back!

The next instant the dog yelped in pain, leaped back on his hind legs and scurried for cover, whining eerily. Lane caught the lightning flash rapidity with which a squat, black snake's head darted back beneath the mouldy trunk. The beady eyes, lidless and glittering, were like phosphorescent shoe-buttons.

Gripping the hatchet handle, Lane circled the reptile's hiding place. He saw it, coiled sleekly in its damp grotto, its shiny, obscene head weaving back and forth, waiting to strike again.

Lane had seen diamond-backs before,

but this was a monster, its thick tail covered with death-sounding rattles. Its pale pink mouth was a slimy hole, and the hollow white fangs curved down over a dripping lower jaw. At intervals, a forked tongue, red as fire, darted out.

Lane crept closer. The pitiful whimpering of the poisoned hound sent shivers through his body. He debated whether to risk a revolver shot at the reptile or use the keen-edged hatchet. If he missed the first shot, the diamond-back would be gone before he could pull the trigger again.

And Lane wanted the snake's head, if only in payment for the venom-tortured hound.

HE poised himself for the moment when that black mottled whip would uncoil and hiss through the air, fangs bared to dig into the flesh of his thigh or leg. But the snake was wary.

Lane came down quietly on his haunches, groped for a tree branch on the forest floor. He found one and held it far to the left, bringing it slowly towards the swaying reptile. The decoy worked. The rattles sounded, and pink mouth gaping, the snake sprang. Lane felt the tug on his left arm as the fangs crunched into the thick branch.

In that split second, Lane swung with the hatchet. Its sharp edge caught the diamond-back inches below its evil head, cut through the muscular body as though it were soft butter. The head, jaws distended, gaped from the ground with motionless ferocity, but the body lashed about in a reflex fury, blood pouring from its severed neck and splashing crimson on the dry, brown fir needles.

Lane sought out the hound, cringing in the brush, its left leg stained red. It would be merciful to put the animal out of its misery. The rattler venom had long since gotten in its murderous work.

Lane drew his gun, placed the barrel opening against the dog's temple. The shot rang out, echoing phantom-like through the forest.

As the last rumble died like the distant boom of thunder, another sound broke the primeval stillness, and brought the woodsman to taut attention. It was the soft scrape of human feet on the yielding fir needles.

Lane ducked behind a tree, the heel of his gun hand resting on his hip. The gloom had deepened and it was difficult to see more than ten feet ahead, but there was no mistaking the swirl of a white skirt and the outline of robust feminine thighs beneath it. A girl!

The realization that a lone girl walked the sombreness of the Black Forest brought to mind Chief Willoughby's statement: ". . . . a curse that's no part of anything human!"

If this forest wanderer was a wraith, Lane decided as she drew closer, she was one damn' good looking apparition! Even with night falling so fast that you could almost feel darkness coming down on you, Lane could see the tawny blonde of her hair, the natural red ripeness of her lips, and most of all, the succulent maturity of her figure beneath her only covering—a thin, cotton dress.

MOMENTARILY he was lost in admiration. Her breasts were deep and full, rising out of her bodice with a firmness that spoke of youth. The upper swells of them, partly visible, were tanned a smooth cream-brown from exposure to the rays of the sun.

The cotton dress, a trifle small for her voluptuous body, clung to the rhythmic flexure of her hips, outlining their lush sweep with amazing fidelity.

As Lane looked on, her deep blue eyes found the still quivering body of the rattler. A cry escaped her lips. She dropped to her knees on the forest floor, reached for the cobbled tail of the reptile. Something glittered in her hand, but Lane saw the flash only out of the corner of his eye.

He was too busy concentrating on the billowing vent of her bodice, and the twin white and brown breasts it revealed. He could look far down into the shadowed valley of them, almost see the sea-shell - sleekness of her curved stomach.

The butt of the gun sweated his palm. He slipped it into his pocket. No sense pulling a gun on a woman.

She came to her feet quickly, her beautifully unblemished face fear-drawn and white beneath its tan. The time was ripe to put in an appearance, Lane thought. He stepped from behind the tree.

"Good-evening," he said.

The girl started. Her eyes widened as she gaped at him in open-mouthed wonderment. Her breasts heaved emotionally, threatening at each pulsating rise to split their thin covering.

Suddenly she wheeled and ran in the direction from which she had come. Lane overtook her before she had taken four steps. His hand caught her wrist, whirled her around so that she faced him.

"Not very sociable, are you?"

Still no sound emerged from the swollen perfection of her mouth. But her eyes spoke volumes. The contracted pupils were pregnant with terror, the irises shot through with bright darts of fire. She tried to tear away from Lane's grip, but he tightened it.

"I'm not going to hurt you," he said. "I just want to ask you a few questions. You see, I'm a stranger around here and—"

"Then you'd better go away!" Lane was shocked to hear her voice. It throbbed and quivered like the muted G-string of a violin. "You'd better go back!" she repeated.

"Go back where?" He was fishing for some explanation of all this.

Her eyes met his. "Wherever you came from. It's dangerous here at night."

Lane laughed softly. "Wild animals?" he queried with a sarcastic intonation. "Wild animals like you?"

"No." Her voice dropped even lower than its natural pitch, faded almost to a whisper. "Snakes!"

He pointed to the diamond-back's stiffening body. "Yes, I just killed it."

A tremor shot through her. "You . . . killed . . . it?"

"Yes. What makes you tremble so?"

She relaxed, her shoulders drooping, but the motion of her splendid breasts still marked her internal excitement. "Don't ask me anything," she gasped. "Just go!"

LANE recalled that something had glittered in her hand when she kneeled down beside the snake's body. He noted her left hand tightly clenched; so much so that the knuckles showed dead white through the brown skin.

"What's in your left hand?" he questioned. Again the tremor electrified her.

"No! Let me go!" Her high-pitched scream broke the Black Forest quietude, seemed to weave in and out between the spectral branches of the giant firs.

Lane grabbed her free wrist, twisted it hard. Her body lurched against him, soft breasts flattened to his chest, the warmth of her thighs piercing even the whipcord material of his breeches.

She fought like a wild-cat to break loose, but eleven years in the Rockies had given Lane Wilbur muscles of drawn steel. A cry of pain escaped her lips as he turned her arm in its socket.

Slowly her fingers opened and a thin gold chain dropped from their aching numbness to the ground. Lane relaxed his grip, but still held her close enough so that he could feel her throbbing bosom. The warmth and fullness of the firm hillocks quickened his own heart beat and sent the blood racing hotly through his veins.

The exotic scent of her vibrant flesh eddied up from the cleft between her breasts, carrying with it a sensual stimulation that was heady physical wine.

It was already too dark to see the feminine ripeness that was so rapturously soft against him, but Lane's sense of touch was keen enough to appreciate each quivering hill and each undulating valley of her figure.

"I'm not going to hurt you unless you force me," he whispered huskily. "Just take it easy."

Her tensed muscles softened and she slumped. Lane dropped her wrists and slipped supporting hands under her arms. He could feel the resiliency of her breasts beneath his thumbs.

Then, like a bolt out of the blue, her arms came up, her hands shot out, and Lane found himself stumbling back. He tripped over the rotted tree trunk, landed on his back. When he scrambled to his feet, he ripped an electric torch from his back pocket and shot its beam of light into the darkness. The girl was gone!

Lane flashed the light on the ground. It caught the sparkle of the thin gold chain. He picked it up, dropped it into his pocket.

The Black Forest was a yawning chasm ahead, beckoning because it had swallowed the girl, and repelling because of the unknown dangers lurking in its inky midst. But the lure of uncanny

Something glittered in the girl's hand.
The rattler still quivered.

mystery was too strong to resist. Lane held his breath, hoping to catch sounds of the girl's retreat.

He heard the faint, far-away snap of a twig. It was enough. Shading the torch lens with his hand, he plunged into the jungle.

TEN minutes of slow travel through the unchartered pitch convinced Lane his quarry was far more familiar with the Black Forest than he. No longer did he hear the noises of movement marking her flight.

He had to depend solely on the physical trail she left, and that was none too clear under artificial light. But still he carried on, wondering what the ultimate goal would be.

The girl had mentioned *snakes!* Chief Willoughby had spoken of a man and a bloodhound pack found dead from rattler bites in these same woods! Was that to be his fate?.

At what moment would he hear the ghastly death rattle, at what moment feel bony fangs sinking into his flesh, and icy venom from a constricted poison sac pouring into his blood-stream?

Once, Lane had seen a man die from a rattler bite. It was a hideous thing to watch. The flesh became livid, then green. Convulsions seized the body. It all ended in a lurid, delirious agony. God, it was horrible!

Too late to think about it now. If death was to come that way, let it come. He transferred the torch to his left hand and brought his revolver to his right. At least, when it *did* come, he'd go down fighting!

A natural arch of fallen trees loomed in front of him. Lane bathed it in light. The mat of fir needles neath it was disturbed, pointing, as clearly as an arrow, the trail the girl had taken. Ahead was more forest, more tangled undergrowth.

Each tree trunk cast its own spectral shadow, each bush loomed out of the darkness like a ghoulish phantom. Shadowed figures seemed to dart out of the inky depths; shrouded shades that floated through the tree branches with ectoplasmic transparency.

Lane took a firmer grip on his gun. He knew these uncanny things were figments of the imagination, meaningless figures created by his own torch, but still the bleak eeriness of them brought chill sweat to his brow.

Suddenly, as though to mock the very confidence his knowledge was giving him, guttural mouthings seeped out of the forest, joining with the flitting wraiths to form a terrifying portent of evil.

LANE stopped short. His heart pounded against his ribs and the tips of his fingers went cold as ice. That sound—part moan, part maniacal chuckle —was no product of his own mind! It was real! It came from a living throat— animal or human!

Again it sounded, and with it came the swish of feet on the fir needle carpet. The beam of light swung in a wide arc as Lane's nervous hand guided it. Something seemed to be moving straight ahead. Lane held the light steady. Yes! *Yes!* A figure was creeping out of the black, coming towards him!

If it were human, the white beam of the torch was twisting it into a hideous travesty of man! Its head melted out of a flat temple and came to a bald, shimmering point a foot above the hollow sockets of its eyes! Its shoulders were hunched—!

What was this creeping, crawling thing whose lips were livid gashes in a hell-spawned face, whose nose was flattened until only hairy holes marked the nostrils, whose body was a gnarled mockery of human shape under a pointed skull so weird as to defy the wildest stretches of imagination? Did it exist? Did it live?

Lane asked himself these questions as the *thing* advanced, its lips drawn back over foul green teeth, the spittle-soaked sucking of its breath a hissing warning.

Lane leveled his gun. If it lived, a bullet would end its fiendish existence. If not—! Thunder and forked fire belched from the revolver, but the *thing* seemed to sense danger.

It became a weaving, shadowed target, creating, by its motions, other shadows to make the forest alive with murky wraiths. The shrieking pellet of lead missed its mark and thudded into a tree trunk.

Lane fired again, pumping the slug at what he thought was the creature. A spine-chilling gurgle answered the boom of the gun, and still the grume-eyed *thing* came forward.

THE cold, clammy fingers of fear fastened on Lane's throat. What manner of mad, inhuman torture was this? The beast was impervious to bullets, impossible to kill! It came on and on, its lips that were not lips curled in a bestial leer. Kill it! *Kill it!* The command shrieked through Lane's mind.

His finger clicked spasmodically on the gun trigger. The forest became alive with the thunder of four shots. Flame spewed from the hot muzzle, winging lead messengers on their way.

And still the creature drew nearer! *God!* Terrified to the point where his muscles were stone, Lane stood rooted to the spot, breath bated and horror-stricken eyes fastened on the malformed monstrosity.

When it was bare feet away, it crouched low. Then, with a spitting snarl, it leaped!

The moment its clammy hands touched Lane's face, the spell of immobility was broken. He fought back with the mad fury of one who has seen the bottomless pit of death; of one who clings to life if only to escape the torture of dying.

Down to the soft floor of the forest they went, the creature snarling and clawing, Lane beating him off as best he could.

But ghastly terror was the *thing's* henchman. More than the hot drool of saliva on Lane's face, more than the bony pressure of slimy fingers on his throat, fright—raw, cutting fright—took its toll of Lane's strength.

He beat the shapeless mask of a face hanging over him, but conscious effort did not guide his blows. He felt himself sinking into the maw of unconsciousness, as gripping fingers bore down on his wind-pipe, forcing precious air from his lungs in great, painful gasps.

But above the delirious hum of motors, above the unceasing pounding at the base of his skull, Lane heard a voice! He had heard that voice only one place before! He whipped his tired brain into thinking of it . . . placing it! *Yes!* In the Black Forest where he had killed the diamond-back! It was the girl's voice! Darkness engulfed him, sucked him down . . . down . . . down. . . .

ROY ELKINS' baby kidnaped . . . Twenty years ago the same crime committed against his father . . . Colonel Matt Elkins . . . Seven babies kidnaped since then . . . All from branches of the circus man's family . . . Queer . . . Colonel Matt big man in Little River . . . No enemies . . . Whole town mourned when he died . . . All friends of Colonel Matt . . . Curse . . . Inhuman curse. . . .

Lane Wilbur fought himself back through the gray morass of insensibility; a dusky swamp peopled with whirling dervishes of thought. He felt pain and knew he was alive. It was an effort to open leaden eyes, but he forced the lids apart.

A familiar face hovered above him. He blinked dazedly, wondering whether it was all a mirage. The face . . . the face . . . it was the *girl's* face! Lane forced a wan smile. His lips shaped.

"Hello," he whispered.

She came down low and the tip of a

(Continued on page 114)

Out of the

The girl leaped up from the couch as the Black One went down in a swirl of cloth.

vealed, desolate and grim.

Even the turbulent, choppy waters of Chesapeake Bay came out of the darkness for one blinding second, its storm-wracked surface reflected in an eerie blue light. Then the night again, dropping over them like a pall, fierce with driving rain.

Between crashes of thunder, came the

THUNDER rolled from the black heavens; cold rain swept over empty sodden fields. In the jagged flashes of blue lightning Bert Martin saw the lonely sweep of Bayhead Island re-

TOMB

By
CHARLES R. ALLEN

A young girl braves prowling vampires where the Dark Angel of Terror rules the haunts of the dead

purr from the sixteen-cylinder sedan, gliding like a black wraith along the winding ribbon of concrete that skirted the bay.

"It's got me!" Martin muttered. "No matter how I twist it around in my head, I can't made any sense from that note!"

Ramos Costigo, driver of the expensive sedan, kept his handsome Spanish face glued to the road ahead, but murmured aside: "Are you sure you read it correctly?"

"Positive! Listen again—there were just two typewritten lines that said:

There will be no moon tonight. He will come out of the minaret tomb in Grayson's cemetery. He will wait for you.

"Strange," murmured Costigo. "And you say this girl, Helen Stone, seemed terrified when she read it?"

"Terrified was no word for it! She almost fainted in my arms—me—a complete stranger to her!"

Martin glanced covertly at the tall, sleek man beside him as he said this. "After all," he wondered privately. "Perhaps this Costigo thinks I'm crazy—coming to him with such a weird tale at this time of night and dragging him out in this storm."

A swift survey of his companion's face, however, gave Martin no hint of what thoughts may lie behind it. Ramos Costigo, imperturbable, bland, wealthy hotel owner and playboy, appeared to have that faculty of complete concentration on the matter in hand. At the moment his entire attention was devoted to the curving, rain-swept road.

"Well," he began suddenly. "As long as we can keep Miss Helen Stone's car in sight, I fancy she will lead us to a solution."

MARTIN'S blue eyes were keen, but it was only by peering intently through the streaming windshield that he could still see the tiny red tail light from the girl's coupe, far ahead of them. Like a ghostly, elfin lantern it moved silently over the barren stretches of Bayhead Island, creeping ever closer to Grayson's Cemetery.

"Perhaps," said Martin, "I haven't made clear enough my own connection with tonight's business. What I told you back at the hotel I had to say in a hurry, for this girl was going out to her car then. You see, it all happened less than an hour ago—all at once, you know. Here I was—a newspaperman on a vacation. Came to Bayhead Hotel for a rest—heard it was nice and quiet.

"Well, I was in my room, undressed, ready for bed, when I heard a girl scream in the room adjoining. At first I wasn't going to pay any attention, for these people at the Bayhead are all pretty swanky and I felt out of place, more or less.

"It was their business if they wanted to go about at nights screaming. But there was something about that scream that made me shiver. I began to wonder. Then I dressed and went into the hall.

"I was just in time to see the next door open and some old guy step out. He beat it—quick—but it was his face that made me decide to investigate. He looked like a dead man—face white as chalk—a dead white, you know. And he acted queer—walked away as though he were in a trance.

"There wasn't a sound from that room since the girl had screamed. And the corridor was deserted, too, after the old man had disappeared. I suppose I was the only one to hear it. That east wing, where those rooms are, is pretty empty right now. I knocked on the door and heard someone whisper—'who's there?'

"I'm not much on etiquette when I'm curious, so I barged right in and there was this Helen Stone dame sitting on the bed with nothing on but a lace negligee."

MARTIN paused, lit a cigarette, as the sedan purred on through the night. His eyes grew wistful over the picture Helen Stone had made, every curve of her lovely body coyly revealed beneath that wispy covering of lace.

Even yet, the glowing memory of two smooth legs, exquisite expressions of feminine grace, gripped him warmly. And her breasts! Proud—scornful of covering, a glory in their naked prominence! Martin sighed.

"I'd seen her before once or twice, understand. But never like that? She was

—well—skip it! She just stared at me, surprised as I was. I saw she was all broken up—crying and sobbing, and her eyes—well they looked as though they'd seen a ghost. Like a kid in a dark house, crazy with fear.

"I went soft over it. I closed the door, walked over, tried to console her. But she wouldn't tell me what was wrong or who that wild lookin' guy was who had left her room as I came in the hall. She just kept on sobbing and telling me to leave. I gave it up and had just started to go when that note came sliding under the door jamb!

"It took me by surprise, snaking under there like that. I stood there and stared for a moment—too long, I suppose, for when I yanked the door open there was no one there! I couldn't help reading it —it stared me right in the face:

There will be no moon tonight. He will come out of the minaret tomb in Grayson's cemetery. He will wait for you.

"I admit it gave me the creeps. But she had come over and read it over my shoulder and she went all to pieces! Just folded up—sobbing and half hysterical. When I tried to help her she pushed me out—told me to go.

"I went to my room, lit up a pipe and tried to figure it out. Then I heard some-one running down the corridor. I looked out. There she was, dressed this time, and on her way downstairs."

"So," interrupted Ramon Costigo, "you came direct to me."

"Exactly. You were the hotel man-ager and I felt there was hell brewing somewhere and that I should follow that girl. Lucky for me you had your car ready and knew where Grayson's Ceme-tery was!"

THE purring black sedan was rolling past a cluster of houses now—Bay Village, Martin knew it to be—a fishing settlement perched on the remote north-ern end of the island. From here the sleek powerful car began to climb a wind-ing hill, leading up to a wind-torn sum-mit overlooking the bay, where lay the desolate, gloomy tombstones that marked Grayson's Cemetery.

Grimly alone, this ancient burial ground nestled forlornly under the sweep of skies on the very crest of the lonely island. The few weather-beaten houses scattered about the section seemed in their drear silence to be themselves abodes of the dead.

Angry streaks of lightning flooded the graveyard intermittently in a spectral light; caught the sagging tombstones for a moment in a bluish, phosphorescent haze, lent an eerie quality to the creep-ing gloom of the place. Far above, the elfin red tail light of the girl's coupe winked out abruptly.

"She's pulled up at the cemetery," muttered Costigo. He gave Martin a quick side glance. "Before you go on with this, perhaps I should mention the strange rumor connected with Grayson's Cemetery."

Martin lit another cigarette. "What's that?"

"The story comes to me second-hand. of course, and is probably no more than legend. But the old fishermen back in the village there, believe it. Not one of them, for all the gold in the world, would come near this place after sunset."

"Why?"

"Vampires, my friend!"

"Vampires—? On Bayhead Island?"

"Bayhead Island," went on the Span-iard, "was one of the first islands inhabi-ted along the Chesapeake. It is old—

very old, and there is a story of a family from India who settled here long ago. Men died mysteriously—their life's blood drained. A reign of terror, on a small scale, existed here.

"But the real terror did not come until this man of India died and supposedly was buried in Grayson's Cemetery. Since then, men have still died strangely in years gone past, and it was said this man was seen walking at night in the grave-yard, among the tombs, seeking human blood. He was undead—a vampire!"

"Rot!" snorted Martin. "Story book stuff!"

"Perhaps," agreed the Spaniard easily. "I have never seen this apparition my-self, of course, but there are some of the old fishermen still living who claim to have seen him—against the sky in the sunset glow."

"And he sends typewritten notes," jeered Martin, "to young girls in the Hotel Bayhead to come out and meet him! Blah!"

COSTIGO smiled. "It is easy to see you are not of the old world. In present-day India and Egypt the exist-ence of human vampires is not doubted. It is so strange that one should find his way to a lonely island in another coun-try? After all, our world is tiny and there are strange things under the sun—things that no one dare explain. But—" he concluded abruptly—"I see you think me a fool. I have simply repeated the tale as I heard it—in case you—"

"It'll take a fast vampire to put me out," grinned Martin. "A two-fisted vampire, with dynamite in both dukes!"

Costigo laughed tolerantly, nosed the sedan off the road into a shallow ditch and doused the lights. Soaked by the driving rain, the two men climbed a low

stone wall, sloshed through the mud of the cemetery.

In a streak of vivid lightning Martin saw the girl, her body bent almost double as she advanced among the tombstones, fighting the storm every inch of the way.

An instant later he spotted the minaret tomb. There was no mistaking it. The only one of its kind here, it stood out in-congruously, a squat structure of white basalt from all four corners of which rose thin Oriental minarets. "The tomb of the Indian vampire," murmured Costigo.

Martin grunted and, with head bowed, moved stolidly in its direction. Nearly blinded by lashing rain, he tripped over a headstone, sprawled flat in the mud and came up dripping, to discover he had lost Costigo in the darkness.

He bawled out the Spaniard's name. Only rain and thunder answered and in the storm-wracked darkness he could see nothing but dim white blurs that marked the sunken, toppled gravestones.

A sudden blinding flash of lightning dazzled him. In its eerie light he took one step forward, then froze. Not ten feet away a black figure stood among the tombs, watching him! Martin saw a ghastly white face, the bony highlights limned clearly in the sudden brilliance.

The man from the hotel! The strange old man who had glided away so silently when he had come out in the hallway!

In the still, quaking flashes of blue light Martin lunged toward him, only to bring up empty handed on the spot where the white-faced one had been.

An icy thrill crawled up his spine as he stood there alone, staring into the blackness. The silent watcher had dis-appeared, whisked away like a formless wraith.

GROPING, cursing, Martin plowed on toward the minaret tomb, the un-

canny spell of the place chilling his blood.
Like a creeping miasma the night closed
around him, swallowed him up.

Terror lurked like a dark angel behind
every pale tombstone; death rode in the
storm-torn air, heavy with menace. Martin dug his nails into the palm of his
hand, stared unseeingly into that dripping, black void from where hundreds of
malignant eyes seemed to watch him.

Costigo was gone, he told himself—
spirited away as completely as though the
graves had opened to receive him! And
that pallid faced one who walked like a
ghost among the tombs—who was he?

Pondering this question, Martin halted. A massive white blur loomed before
him. He shouted: "Costigo!" then re-
coiled violently as an answering scream

Together they
crawled through
the aperture to
the stone floor
above.

split the silence—a girl's scream, high-pitched, shrieking, quavering in terror.

Lightning crackled across the sky, lighted the graveyard brilliantly for a moment. Martin gasped. Directly before him was the white basalt of the minaret tomb and on its threshold stood a tall, lean man draped from head to foot in black cloth. In his arms was the struggling, slicker-clad form of Helen Stone.

Even while he watched in stunned amazement Martin saw the Black One encircle the girl's waist with his long arms, lift her bodily from the steps, throw her through the black, yawning doorway of the tomb.

The lightning winked out and Martin plunged snarling through the darkness, hard fists doubled up, ready for action. He crashed into the three stone steps that led to the vault door, smashed his shin.

Unheeding the pain, he scrambled up, lashed out a terrific blow. Hard stone greeted his knuckles, scraped them. His other fist swung around, swished through empty air.

Then, as though all the fury in the heavens had converged in one tremendous smash, something cracked on his head with shattering force. Circles of light exploded in his brain. Then blackness, silent and unmoving.

CENTURIES later, it seemed, his eyes flickered open. He was lying face down in a mud puddle, his clothes sodden; his head raging like an inferno. Like a drunken man he swayed to his feet, blue eyes narrowed in impotent rage.

Cold rain lashed his mud streaked face as he stared around. There was no spectral, dark-robed figure on the steps of the minaret tomb now, nor anywhere else near by. The place was deserted, literally, as a graveyard.

Weird fancies gripped him. Was it a nightmare, or had Costigo really been spirited away before his eyes and the charming Helen Stone dragged, screaming, into a tomb by a sinister shadow? Martin rubbed the bump on his head ruefully. There wasn't anything shadowy about that blow, or the strength behind it.

What was it Costigo had said about a human vampire? Vaguely Martin recalled tales he had heard concerning vampires—of their weird cunning; their ferocious strength.

Shaking his head as one throwing off a bad dream, he advanced to the minaret tomb, ran an exploring hand over the massive steel door. He found it tightly shut, with no indication it had ever been open. Further search revealed a tiny, iron-barred window, high up on the east wall.

To get in or out of that would be impossible. Nothing for it but to find Costigo's car, get back to town and bring men and tools; force the grim vault to give up its secret.

Fuming inwardly, Martin sloshed away through the mud. Bowing his aching head before the storm, he had gone two or three hundred yards before he realized he was walking away from the road—in fact, had left the limits of the cemetery altogether and was beginning to descend the southern side of the hill.

He turned, mumbling a disgruntled curse, and saw for the first time a rambling black pile a few yards to his left.

A sixth sense of danger made him advance slowly, cautiously. The pile gradually took the vague outlines of a house —a dark, sinister, shuttered house, as bleak and lifeless as the cemetery he had just quitted.

Curiously, Martin walked around it, saw it was dilapidated; gone to seed, with sagging wooden steps, rotting walls and broken shutters. In the rear he found what had once been a garden, now a rank jungle of tall grass, weeds and dead vines.

MARTIN shrugged, turned back. Then, with a crash that rose above the rain and thunder, came the unmistakable noise of shattering glass; the beginning of a feminine scream—a scream that was choked off abruptly.

Like a flying shadow Martin went up the sagging back steps in two bounds. A faint tinkle of tumbling glass still echoed from the darkness. Someone had smashed the rear porch window from within!

With the lovely vision of Helen Stone before him and the echo of a cry that had sounded like hers still in his ears, he fumbled with a crazy shutter, found a crevice where two slats were missing, closed both hands over it and yanked. The shutter came off with a dreadful screeching of rusty bolts, like the tortured scream of a lost soul.

In the panting blackness Martin waited tensely. Before him was a broken, jagged window—a gaping hole beyond which lay Stygian gloom, silent and foreboding.

When the unbroken silence told him no one was coming he climbed carefully over the glass strewn windowsill, lowered himself to a creaking wooden floor. Step by step he inched through the darkness, sliding his hand along a rough wall until he had glided through a doorway and into a narrow hall.

Under his breath he cursed as the wet mud on his boots squished at every step. A low-pitched voice came to him now from the far end of the hall; a voice sinister in quality, monotonous in its chant-like inflection.

From the room whence it issued, flickering light threw ghostly, dancing shadows out in the hall. Martin watched their grotesque play for a moment as they vainly tried to diffuse the gloom of this drab, empty house. Then, on his toes, he slid forward, hugging the wall.

Reaching the doorway of a lofty but bare living room, he gambled a quick glance. The tableau within shot his eyes wide open. On a rough wooden table was an empty bottle from the neck of which a guttering candle sent out its feeble expiring rays.

The shadowy light wavered over a strangely assorted trio: on a frayed sofa the black-robed and hooded figure Martin had last seen on the steps of the minaret tomb, leaned menacingly over Helen Stone, his fingers wound about her white throat.

The girl was stripped down to her lace step-ins and a gauzy brassiere, her gleaming white body stretched flat on the sofa, and on her face the twisted expression of fear and loathing. On a chair against the wall sat another man, old, white of face with graying hair.

The same man, Martin realized, he had seen under the lightning's flash, standing among the tombs, watching him. His white face was now totally expressionless; his movements those of a man hypnotized. Every few seconds he lifted a cigarette to his gray lips, dreamily exhaled a cloud of smoke and watched without interest the writhing, sinuous body of Helen Stone.

FASCINATED by the macabre scene, Martin's eyes swung back to the girl; to the little pile of clothes that lay at her feet—dress, slip, shoes, and stockings.

Her gleaming legs, pink and white columns of alluring girl-flesh, kicked and twisted under the grip of the Black One; brought into play rich movements of her curving thighs that even in this danger-laden moment warmed Martin's blood. The hand of the Black One slid over her flat stomach, across her abdomen and grisped the frilly edge of her brassiere.

"You see," he muttered thickly, "it is as easy as this." With one savage yank he ripped away the feminine garment. Swelling white breasts appeared, firm and lovely in their snowy nakedness.

Martin caught his breath as he watched those vibrant mounds sway wildly with the twistings of her body, but he stood his ground, waiting for a chance remark that might give him the key to the riddle.

The Black One, however, was more intent on action than words. His hands cupped the girl's pointed breasts, lingered there caressingly. Then with sadistic deliberation he quit them, moved his fingers along her swelling thighs to the elastic rim of the step-ins.

Martin saw the dent in her soft stomach as his hand toyed with the silk cloth. . . . "It is useless," growled her tormentor, "to struggle. You cannot stop me! Others have tried—and failed. Either get for me what I ask—or this—"

SAVAGELY he ripped at the step-ins. The girl's eyes rolled in desperation, her white body arched upward in a last attempt to throw off the attacker. Martin leaped like a muddy ghost out of the gloom, flying across the room, head lowered, arms oustretched.

He struck the hips of the Black One at full speed, just as the latter's body was descending toward the naked girl. The two men crashed on the end of the couch, fell with a thud to the bare floor.

Martin's hard fists played a tattoo on the man beneath him, driving in short powerful blows to stomach, chest, and head. His opponent wrapped long legs about Martin's hips, dug sinewy fingers into his throat, forced him over.

Kicking and lashing, Martin tore himself free, lunged a right swing at the hooded attacker that drove him backward. He came to his feet; smashed home another right; felt it crack dully on a jawbone.

The Black One went down in a swirl of black cloth, but seeming to sense inevitable defeat, rolled over once, scrambled up and shot out the door like a flying black shadow.

Helen Stone climbed from the couch, clinging desperately to her one remaining garment. "Stop him!" she gasped. "Don't let him get away!"

Martin stared for a moment at the seductive play of a candlelight dancing over her soft white body. He saw, too, that the white-faced man in the corner had risen, the cigarette still dangling from his lips and on his features a vacuous, uncomprehending expression. Then he whirled, plunged toward the dark hallway.

Pattering over the bare floor behind him came the naked feet of the girl. "The cellar door!" she called out. "He'll go that way!"

MARTIN ploughed through his damp pockets, came out with a match that would still light. In its tiny flare they saw a deserted kitchen, in the far wall of which a decrepit door stood partly ajar.

Over its threshold Martin stared down a flight of crazy steps, deep in gloom. The girl's hand slipped into his. "He—he mustn't get away. I came here to unmask him. He—"

Martin grabbed her, started down the

stairs. "Come on sister! If he's hiding here, I'll find him!"

In the cellar, rats scampered away before their approach, their little red eyes

He lifted and threw her bodily.

shining like evil fires. "The tunnel!" whispered Helen Stone. "He's probably gone through the tunnel. He'll get away!"

"What tunnel?"

"At the end of the cellar—a trapdoor. He brought us in that way!"

The girl's sinuous, unclad body was close against him now, her soft flesh quivering in the dampness. Instinctively, Martin threw an arm about her waist and his fingers brushed the tip of one curving breast. She shivered.

They found the trap door finally—a

carefully cut slab in the cellar floor with a small iron ring as its handle. A pile of rubbish shoved to one side was mute evidence that some one had used it quite recently.

Martin yanked it up, saw a yawning black hole. "Jump!" whispered Helen. He jumped, landed on boggy earth, caught the girl's descending body in his arms.

"Holy mackerel, sister! This is no place for you—without a stitch of clothes on!" Hastily he shed his raincoat, slid it over her aluring curves. "That doesn't matter now!" Her tone was sharp, shot with desperation. "Nothing will matter if we don't stop him!"

"O. K. But who is he?"

"I don't know."

Surprised, Martin waited for further information, but receiving none shrugged his shoulders, started to move forward.

In this underground passage the air was foul with the rot of centuries. His feet slithered through deep slime and the curving walls he slid his hands along were thick with greasy moisture.

"If I believed in vampires," he called back, "I'd sure expect to find them in a place like this."

VAMPIRES?" The girl seemed startled. Martin heard her uneven breathing as she labored through the tunnel after him. Then abruptly, she spoke: "I'll tell what happened. You deserve to know. That man we left back there is my father."

"Your father! The white-faced man?"

"Yes. Andrew Stone, the banker."

"But—" protested Martin.

"I know what you're thinking," she interrupted swiftly. "You're wondering why he sat there and did nothing while that—that monster—was—"

"Exactly!"

"Well, he couldn't do anything! The cigarette he was smoking was full of hasheesh—dope of the worst sort! He was in a trance!"

"So that's it!"

"That's only half! You see, the man in black, whoever he is, discovered somehow that my father was involved, through no fault of his own, in a banking scandal—a big one—a terrible thing. Months ago he began to blackmail father —sent him notes at first and signed them *The Black One.*

He had father meet him in this place and pay over blackmail. At first it was small amounts, then each time he wanted more. Father tried to find out who he was, but always failed. He had no other choice but to pay—this man knew everything and threatened exposure and jail."

"When he began to demand huge sums, father refused. Then he brought out this dope scheme—" Her voice broke for a moment in utter hopelessness and Martin became conscious of a flowing wave of pity. "His plan was simple," she went on bitterly.

"He forced my father, at gun point, to smoke these cigarettes with hasheesh in them. Gradually his will weakened, he became helpless and paid whatever this man asked. Worst of all, the stuff got a hold on him and he even began to want it!"

MARTIN'S burly fist clenched tight. "If we find that clever gent," he promised grimly, "He'll have to put a mask over his face from now on! He'll need it. Besides, I've an account to settle myself—he laid out the chap that brought me here—Ramos Costigo—did away with him!"

"I knew father was in some sort of trouble," the girl continued swiftly. "I came to live at the Bayhead, where he was, and made him tell me. I took a room further down the hall, pretended there was no relation between us, so I would be free to spy on this blackmailer."

"I didn't find out much, and tonight I was worried because father seemed so downcast. Just before I was ready to get in bed I decided to run up and see him. When I came in I saw him about to kill himself with a revolver. I screamed and stopped him. We talked it over and made him go out for a walk and promise to calm down. Then you came in."

"So!" grunted Martin. "That explains why that bird slid his note under the door. He saw a light there and thought your father was in!

"Yes. I took the note to father. I knew he would go to meet him, even without taking the usual amount of cash along. You see, I had taken all the cash he had left and hidden it in a safe place. Father didn't know this, of course. Well, I was desperate.

"I followed him to the cemetery. He hid his car behind some shrubbery and went up to that vault. I went after him. I was too anxious, I suppose, to find that blackmailer—tear his mask off. Perhaps if we knew who he was it might have helped. I made too much noise and before I could help myself he had me in the vault.

"He had a gun. and he took both of us through a trap door in the vault floor and made us go though this passageway that ends in the empty house. He doped father, tried to force me to tell where I had hidden the money by—by—"

"I," observed Martin grimly, "saw what he was doing. But that's all over. The trouble now—" He paused, having reached a blank, slimy wall. "Looks

like we draw a blank, sister! How he ever discovered this old passageway beats me. but he appears to know his way about pretty well."

"He's gone!" whispered the girl, her voice heavy with tragedy. "And father—"

"We might catch him before he gets out of the cemetery. Where's the trap door—ah!" Martin grunted as his fingers found a series of crevices cut into the sloping side wall. Clambering up, he shoved against roof, felt a stone slab move upward. Through the dim aperture came a gust of musty air and rolling crash of thunder from the outer world.

HE gripped the bare armpits of Helen Stone, helped her up. Together they crawled out on the stone floor of the minaret tomb. A streak of blue lightning crackled outside the high iron-barred window, lit up the grim, bare tomb for an instant in an eerie light.

Almost simultaneously came the thunderous crash of a revolver as a tongue of orange flame stabbed the gloom. A slug shrieked across the vault, missed Martin's head by inches.

In the crashing echoes of the shot, Helen Stone screamed. Martin lunged toward the spot from where flame had spurted, smashed headlong into a retreating figure. Frantically he groped for the gun hand, found it and wrenched savagely.

His unseen opponent spat out an oath as the gun was torn from his fingers and sent flying across the floor. A steel-muscled hand shot out, gripped Martin's throat. Martin responded promptly with a terrific, smashing blow to the other's stomach.

Lightning snaked through the vault again as the injured man gasped in pain,

(Continued on page 121)

BRIDE of the

Deity or emblem of incarnate evil? What is it? Sandra knows only that she cannot resist its hypnotic eyes.

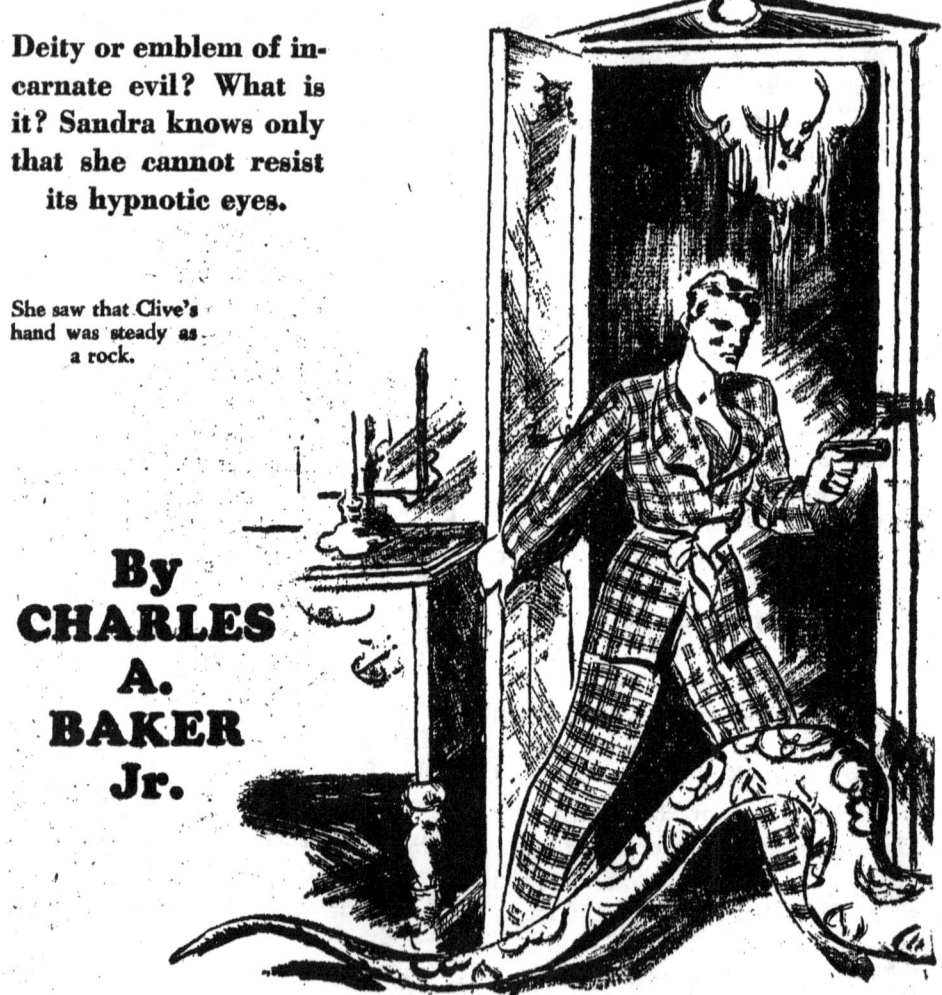

She saw that Clive's hand was steady as a rock.

By
CHARLES
A.
BAKER
Jr.

IT WAS his eyes that fascinated Sandra, strange, ruddy, serpentine eyes, with oval, vertical pupils, eyes mysterious and terrible, filled with wisdom and a sort of brooding evil. She could feel them watching her, fixed on her, gloating over her, as a cat gloats over a bird. A shudder ran over her, icy cold; a premonition of evil that she could not dispel.

Malik Stevenson was a handsome man.

Clive had told her that he must be at least fifty, but he might have passed for thirty. There was no grey in his thick black hair, and there were no wrinkles on his pale skin. His thin lips were very red. His teeth were white and even, but extraordinarily long, so that when he smiled, his canines showed like fangs.

And there was something weirdly serpentine about him: his long, lean figure, the easy, flowing grace of his motions.

SERPENT

His hands moved with the darting quickness of a snake's head. Like a serpent, he both attracted and repelled Sandra.

The place was filled with serpents. On the thick tapestries that covered the walls, and muffled the roaring of the storm outside, golden and silver snakes writhed, snakes black and green and golden. The sullen splendor of the great oriental rug that covered the hardwood floor was snake-patterned.

The huge marble mantle-piece was supported by two entwined serpents. The iron fire-tongs were serpentine in form. The massive silver chandelier was a

many-headed serpent. And the candles that burned in it were like pallid, rigid snakes, that became more serpentine still when they began to droop.

The night was not cold, but a mighty fire roared in the cavernous fire-place, so that the immense room was filled with a stifling, tropical heat. And the heated air was heavy with some strange, musky scent, at once alluring and repulsive.

Everything about Malik's enormous house was sumptuous, magnificent, beautiful, but with an unholy, venomous, and sinister beauty, a beauty that repelled as much as it attracted. Sandra Stevenson could understand, now, why the natives had acted so strangely when asked the way to this household, why they had muttered something about "sorcery."

IT WAS the first time either Sandra or her husband had ever seen the latter's distant cousin Malik. Since they had happened to be motoring in the neighborhood, they had decided to call, and he had insisted that they spend the night. He was, Clive had told her, something of a mystery. Very little was known about him. There were, to be sure, strange and even ugly rumors, but they were of the most indefinite description.

He had traveled all over the world, acquired great wealth—no one knew how —and he now lived in solitary splendor, in the remotest depths of the country.

He baffled Sandra, more than any man she had ever met. His manners were perfect, he was a brilliant conversationalist, cultivated and well informed on all subjects. But there was an indefinable something about him that frightened her. Somehow, Sandra felt very glad that she was not alone with him.

Those eyes of his seemed to bore right through her clothing, so that she felt herself blushing with an absurd shame, as if she had been naked before him.

"You seem fond of serpents, cousin Malik!" she remarked.

"Serpents fascinate me!" he admitted. "I have studied the cult of serpent worship in many lands. All ages and all peoples have felt that there was some-

thing supernatural about the serpent, that it has power not possessed by beast or mortal; that it is the representative of superhuman, supernatural forces. The ancients worshiped it as a deity. And has not Christianity made the serpent the supreme emblem of incarnate evil?"

"But how do they worship the serpent?" asked Sandra.

"Oh, in many ways, but chiefly by sacrifice—especially human sacrifice."

Sandra shuddered. "Really? Even today?"

Malik laughed. "Even today! But, of course, you have to have a pretty big snake, to swallow a human being! You'd be surprised, though, if you knew how common such cults really are. An especially acceptable sacrifice to the serpent god, of course, is a beautiful young woman. Like you, for instance!"

Sandra tried to laugh, but her laugh sounded forced and hollow. Somehow, she could find nothing humorous about the idea. In those surroundings, it sounded altogether too plausible for comfort.

Those eyes of Malik's! Would they never stop looking at her? She tried to tear her own away from them, but the harder she tried not to look at them, the more irresistable became the temptation to do so. They fascinated her, almost hypnotized her, filling her with the strangest, the most ineffable mixture of horror and delight.

Those eyes were as old as lust, and cruelty, and all evil—and as young. They were as wise as evil itself, as strong, as terrible, as alluring. They seemed to speak to her, to invite her, to promise her, to threaten her. What they threatened and promised were ineffable torments, and ineffable delights, things wholly accursed, inconceivable, that chilled her with terror, and yet filled her with longing anticipation. Those eyes were branding themselves upon her soul like hot irons.

Sandra shook her head, angrily, trying to clear it. This was ridiculous! The hot, scented air, and the liqueur she had been sipping, strangely bitter-sweet, must have made her dizzy.

Clive yawned, loudly. "My bed-time!" he announced.

"Mine, too!" said Sandra. She wanted to get away from those eyes. To be alone with her husband.

BUT even when Malik left them, at the door of their bedroom, those eyes continued to haunt her. This room, too, was hung with serpentine tapestries, had a serpentine candelabra. It was very hot from the fire on the hearth. And the great, old-fashioned bed had four posts, each carved in the form of a giant serpent entwined around a shrinking woman.

"Strange duck, Malik!" yawned Clive. "God, I'm sleepy!"

His head had no sooner touched the pillow than he fell asleep. But Sandra was prey to a strange sleeplessness. For all the downy softness of the magnificent bed, she tossed restlessly from side to side, listening to the howling of the storm, that seemed rather to increase than to diminish.

Clive had put out the fire, but the embers that still glowed on the hearth reminded her of Malik's eyes. She turned away, but those glowering eyes still seemed to stare at her out of the shadows.

She shivered with fear, pressing her body closer to Clive's. She closed her eyes, sinking down under the covers. But now it seemed to her that she could sense Malik's presence, that he was standing beside the bed looking at her. In vain she tried to reason away the sensation, it grew stronger and stronger. Finally,

she opened her eyes, peering fearfully out from the covers.

There was nothing there. Again Sandra closed her eyes. And immediately she felt again the sensation of being watched by a hostile, brooding presence. Unable to sleep, she raised her lids once more. This time, she almost cried out in terror. A dark, tall form seemed to loom over her, threateningly, with ruddy eyes. But it was only a trick of the shadows, and the ruddy eyes an illusion of her own.

Sandra told herself that she was tired, nervous, and overwrought, that she would be all right in the morning. Sleep was all she needed. But she could not sleep. She found herself staring at the shadowy tapestries on the wall. Their serpents seemed to creep, filled with an uncanny vitality; their eyes glowed in the darkness with a metallic luster, like the eyes of Malik Stevenson.

She found herself trembling with fear, close to tears. The storm was tearing at the windows with demoniac fingers. The howling of it sounded like obscene, fiendish threats. Vividly there came to Sandra's mind the long-forgotten terrors of her childhood, when, on a dark and stormy night, she lay alone in her bed. But now she was no longer a child, or alone. Of what, then, was she afraid?

AT LAST she slept, and a frightful nightmare came to her. A monstrous serpent lay coiled before her, with Malik's face, and Malik's eyes. It crept toward her, open-mouthed, and its terrible eyes held her spell-bound. An awful terror seized on Sandra, an unutterable loathing, mingled with a terrible fascination, an indescribable yearning. She awoke dripping with sweat, and trembling like a leaf.

She still felt that mingled terror and

fascination, yearning and loathing. And she could sense the presence of an ancient and ineffable evil, an invisible, inaudible, intangible horror, that froze her brain, her very blood. Beside her, she could hear Clive's breathing, slow, deep, and regular. But she dared not wake him, dared not utter the slightest sound, dared not move a single muscle, dared not breath.

She seemed to see those terrible, ruddy eyes, the eyes of Satan himself, staring at her out of the darkness. Sandra lowered her lids, but even that did not shut them out, she could still see them, as if they had been burned deep into her brain. They were summoning her.

Sandra's own will was no longer master of her own body. An infinitely stronger will, a well inhuman, evil, irresistible, had taken possession of all her faculties. She could not fight against it, she did not want to fight against it. An unutterable despair had seized her.

She was conscious of what she was doing, or rather of what her body was doing, but she was not doing it. She was not willing her muscles to act as they did. They were acting under the volition of that other, Satanic will.

Quietly, striving not to arouse Clive, she sat up. Softly, she got out of bed. For a moment she stood there, while her slim hands fluttered to her breasts, as if to still the beating of her heart. Then silently, slender and white as a ghost, in her bare feet, she glided towards the door, hands outstretched before her.

Her fingers found the heavy iron bolt, which Clive had shot. It slid back soundlessly, and as soundlessly the door swung open before her. Now she was outside it, moving down the corridor. It was cold there, the night air was chill on her unclad body. But she did not shiver.

It was as if Sandra were observing the actions of another, someone on the stage or screen, someone in whom she was very much interested.

The corridor was bathed with an eery, greyish light, the source of which she could not discover. With every step she took, Sandra's terror of the unknown towards which she was being drawn increased. In vain she fought, with every atom of her will, against that diabolical compulsion.

Invisible cables seemed to be dragging her unwilling feet on irresistibly. Desperately, she strove to convince herself that it was only a dream. But, all along, she knew that she was wide awake.

HOW long Sandra walked, or how far she never knew. It seemed miles and hours, before she pushed open a massive door, and found herself in an immense vaulted chamber, windowless, but bathed in a lurid yellow light. The walls were of jet-black stone, streaked and veined with yellow. The floor was paved with alternate squares of black and yellow stone. The texture of them was slightly rough under her feet. The air was very hot.

At the far end of the room was a magnificent yellow rug. On the rug was something that at first sight, Sandra took for a heap of gorgeous tapestry, yellow and brown and black, shot through with iridescent glowings. Then it moved.

Sandra strove to scream, but no sound issued from her trembling lips. It was a gigantic serpent its body as thick as her own. It raised its great head, flat and triangular and evil, and stared at her out of ruddy, unwinking eyes, eyes cold and hard as gems, the eyes of Malik.

Its monstrous jaws opened, the light glinted on the long white needles of its

The next thing she knew Clive was pouring brandy down her throat.

terrible fangs, and its tongue, forked and scarlet as flame, darted in and out as if it were licking its chops.

The very marrow of Sandra's bones seemed to dissolve in horror and loathing. But those terrible eyes held her fixed, fascinated, hypnotized. They penetrated to the inmost recesses of her soul, drawing her onward as a magnet draws iron filings. In the middle of the floor, she stood still, weak and trembling, waiting. She remembered the stories she had heard of how a snake can fascinate a bird. And she knew that it was even so with her, that it was those awful eyes that had drawn her here.

The serpent began to uncoil its monstrous length, yard on glistening yard, to flow towards her, like an infernal river. She could hear the terrible dry harsh scraping of its scales against the stone. She could see those scales flashing in the yellow light, as it moved. And always it kept its eyes fixed on hers.

Two yards away, it paused. Its head shot upwards, until its body became a swaying column, and its eyes were gazing down into hers. Sandra could smell the musky, sickening reptilian odor of it, overpoweringly strong. The head dropped, the coils lapped, cold as water, around Sandra's feet.

I T WAS lifting itself, a massy coil went around her thighs, another around her hips and her slender waist, another crushed her firm breasts. The rough scales irritated her tender flesh, filling her with an unendurable loathing. But an evil and poisonous excitement was mingled with that loathing, a perverse desire.

The mere weight of the monster's scaly body was crushing. And now that frightful face was only inches from her own. The fetid and nauseating breath of it was in her nostrils, cold saliva dripped from its grim jaws onto her naked flesh. Its tongue licked out, touching her lips in an unholy caress. It hissed, sibilantly.

Those steely coils were beginning to tighten, squeezing the breath from Sandra's slim body, threatening to cave in her ribs. Agonizing pain suffused every fiber of her. She would have screamed, but she could not utter a sound, could not breathe.

In a moment she would lose consciousness, in a moment all the life would be driven out of her. There was a great roaring in her ears, a great blackness in her eyes. And still she saw those fiendish eyes, the eyes of Malik.

The pressure relaxed, the pain eased.

Sandra could breathe again. Her hands went to the back of the serpent's neck. Impelled by she knew not what instinct of submission to an irresistible power, she began to caress it, to fondle it, running her hands all along the length of it from the head down, feeling the scales ruffle under her sensitive fingertips, the ribs swell as it breathed. That mighty body trembled, the serpent hissed in joy.

A cry echoed from the vaulted ceiling. "Sandra!" The serpent lifted its head. For the first time its eyes left hers. And it was as if the spell that bound her had snapped, like a chain. She screamed, and began to struggle.

Twisting her head, she saw Clive, in his pajamas, standing in the doorway, a revolver in his hand, and agony in his eyes.

The serpent's coils had released a little. Now they began to tighten again, cutting off her breath. The serpent hissed, ominously, as if warning her savior off. A sudden hope sprang up in Sandra's breast. Clive, she knew, was a dead shot.

"For God's sake, shoot!" she cried. "Even if you hit me!"

"Don't move!" he snapped.

With a tremendous effort of will, Sandra obeyed. Yet, even then, she knew it was hopeless. Such a huge reptile must have a tremendous tenacity of life. Even if Clive could shatter its head with a single shot, it would crush her body to pulp in its death flurry. She saw Clive's gun hand going out, steady as a rock. It blazed, and a roaring concussion deafened her. Something whistled past her ear, something cold and wet splashed on her shoulder.

Then the coils tightened on her convulsively, and a scalding tide of agony swept away her consciousness.

HER next awareness was of amazement that she was still alive. She was lying on the tiled floor, with Clive bending over her. Every fiber of her ached like fire, to breathe was anguish. But to be alive at all was joy unspeakable.

"Thank God!" Clive was saying. "You're alive! And no ribs broken, even!"

Every word Sandra spoke was an effort. "I still don't see how—"

"You wouldn't be," said Clive, grimly, "if you hadn't left the covers off me, so I woke up, or if your affectionate pal hadn't exposed his throat. I put a bullet through it, shattering his spinal cord at the very top. That's almost instant death to anything with a backbone. But I'm going to tell Mr. Malik a thing or two about the kind of pets he keeps."

Clive turned his head. And then Sandra heard him cry out: "Oh, my God!" He snatched her up in his arms, and sprinted out of that accursed chamber.

"Clive," she protested, "you can't take me out like this! I haven't a thing on!"

But Clive was wasting no breath in words. The jolting was too much for Sandra's poor tortured body. After that she must have fainted again.

The next thing she knew she found herself seated in their car, wrapped in a robe, while Clive poured brandy down her throat. The storm was over, and the eastern sky was already red with the dawn. But the western sky was redder still from the glow from Malik's house, now a mass of flames.

Her own voice seemed to come from a great distance. "Lightning?"

"I guess that will be the official verdict," said her husband. "As a matter of fact, I stopped just long enough to light it."

"I—I don't understand," murmured Sandra.

"Neither do I. And what's more, I don't want to understand. All I know is what I saw on the floor of that room, when I turned around."

"What was that?"

"It wasn't the snake I'd just shot. There wasn't a sign of that. The thing that lay there on the floor was Malik, naked, with a big bullet hole in his throat!"

DEATH VAULT

In the ancient catacombs of Rome are hoary crypts . . .
glass sepulchers of the living dead. What was her fate
—the American girl trapped in the horror chambers?

T HERE were but three passengers
on the Milan-Rome bus as it sped
through the storm-swept night. It
had emptied out considerably at Flor-
ence, and almost completely at the last
stop before Rome, the town of Sienna.
There, the rain had begun coming down

in veritable torrents, beating up against
the sloping olive groves and pouring into
the road like rushing brown rivers.

The bus swayed from side to side as
it took the banked curves of the Via
Empoli, hurtling ahead like an un-
leashed greyhound when the road

She lay as if sleeping,
in the glass case. Was
she dead?

# of VENUS

By ARTHUR WALLACE

straightened. But always it sped on.

In Seats 4 and 5, a pretty blonde girl rested her head on the shoulder of her youthful male companion. Her eyes were closed but it was difficult to conceive that she might be sleeping, in view of the motion of the ponderous vehicle. The young man's arm was about her

waist, his fingers resting lightly on the relaxed curve of her hip. He was peering out the rain-spattered window, trying to pierce the almost impenetrable darkness.

Across the aisle, the third passenger, a middle-aged gentleman possessed of a finely chiseled head, was reading a book.

His detachment from the world without was complete. He read eagerly, devouring each page as a hungry man wolfs bread.

The seat light above him played on the neatly cut sheen of an ebony goatee and mustache, giving them almost onyx brilliancy. Rarely did he lift his eyes from the printed words, and then only to rest them momentarily.

On the passenger list, tacked to a board above the driver's head, the occupants of Seats 4 and 5 were listed as Mr. and Mrs. Hugh Bedford, New York, U. S. A., and the occupant of Seat 6, across the aisle, as Dr. Giovanni Vecchio, Rome. Only the inexorable eye of fate could look down upon these people and see the amazing chain of events that was to weld them indiffusably and bring horror to their souls and pain to their bodies.

UNKNOWING, Dr. Vecchio read on, and Jane Bedford, a bride of three weeks, moved closer to her husband, seeking warmth and the comfort of protection. His hand slid up and found the under-curve of a firm breast. She smiled softly, indicating her pleasure.

Then, suddenly, the bus lurched to one side. Soaked brakes screeched protestingly. The huge body swung to the edge of the road and one double wheel dropped sickeningly into a mud-filled ditch.

The sudden stop and lurch spun Dr. Vecchio from his seat and hurled him across the aisle on top of Jane and Hugh

Bedford. When the bus had settled, he righted himself quickly.

"*Perdoneme, signore e signora.* It was so sudden!"

Hugh Bedford smiled agreement. "Yes, what happened?"

A volley of oaths in Italian emanated from the driver as he slipped from his seat to investigate.

Dr. Vecchio shrugged. "I do not know, *signor,* but to listen to our driver it is the end of the world." For the first time he seemed to notice the pale beauty of Jane Bedford. His eyes, softly magnetic beneath heavy lashes, met her frightened orbs. "There is nothing to fear, *signora.* I feel certain it is nothing but a flat tire. The driver will fix it in very short order and we cannot be far from Rome."

"*Dannazione! Diavalo!*" Soaked to the skin the bus operator scrambled back into the vehicle. "*Nello fango!*" he blurted, water dripping from his chin. "*Non podemos liberarnos!*"

Dr. Vecchio turned to the Americans. "He says that the wheel is stuck in the mud and he cannot liberate it." He queried the driver rapidly, translated his replies. "It is twelve miles to Rome and we are at the beginning of the Via de Porta Sebastiano." He consulted a watch. "It is after midnight and there is little traffic on this road." Liquid vowels rolled off his tongue like the soft lapping of a woodland stream.

"Does that mean we stay here all night?" Hugh queried. "Isn't there some way of reaching Rome?"

Dr. Vecchio shrugged. "None that I know of, *signore.* For myself I do not mind, but I can well understand your concern over the comfort of the charming *signora.*"

Jane shrank from his eyes and yet found herself drawn to them strangely.

They were neither covetous nor sensual, avoiding the pert mounds of her ripening breasts and the lyred curve of her hips, but melting into her face with a paternal idolatry.

Hugh's arm tightened about her waist. "Yes, that's it," he said. "You see, my wife isn't very strong. She's been ill and—and—"

"Of course," Dr. Vecchio nodded. "I understand perfectly. You see, I am a physician—Giovanni Vecchio."

Hugh extended his free right hand. "I'm Hugh Bedford and this is my wife, Jane, Doctor. We're on our honeymoon and this thing rather breaks it up. If we could just—"

"I was about to suggest," Dr. Vecchio interrupted, "that you permit me to be of service to you. I am acquainted with a professional colleague whose home is but a five minute walk from this point."

Something flickered in his eyes. "I had not intended visiting him so suddenly, but since we are virtually marooned here for the night, I feel I can extend you the comfort, if not the courtesy, of his home. It may be possible, from there, to communicate with Rome and arrange for transportation." He turned and removed a raincoat from the rack above his seat. "If the *signora* will use my coat . . . . it is raining quite heavily."

MOMENTS later they were trudging through the storm, leaning forward as they walked to brace their bodies against a high, whipping wind. It was longer than a five minute walk, but finally, around a bend in the road, the bleak turrets of a stone mansion loomed out of the night. Lights burned in a second floor window. The lower floor was dark.

Dr. Vecchio led the way to an arched portico and lifting the iron knocker on the stout front door, let it fall. The sound echoed through the house. Jane shivered and crept into Hugh's arms. Even the atmosphere was charged with a tingling frost. Dr. Vecchio raised and dropped the knocker again. A chain rattled, a bolt slipped through a rusty hasp and the door opened.

Dr. Vecchio motioned Jane and Hugh inside, then followed. The door closed behind them and the dwarfed figure of a man crept out of the shadows. His head was half the size of his midget body, with great, popping eyes, and wolf teeth that slipped over his lower lip, creating a constant evil leer.

"*Salutos,* Ubaldo," Dr. Vecchio greeted. "You will tell your master that I am here with two friends."

Jane, petrified at sight of the deformed human, grew pale and swayed against Hugh. As the dwarf moved across the floor, his footsteps rang through the high-vaulted, beamed ceiling. *Boom! Boom! Boom!* Like the beat of savage tom-toms.

"A strange house," Dr. Vecchio said, "and a stranger owner. I wish to prepare you both for Dr. Cagliostro. He is by no means a handsome man. An unfortunate accident during a chemical experiment obliterated most of his features. Only through the skill of plastic surgeons was his face brought back to some human semblance. However, he has a brilliant mind and—"

He paused abruptly as a tall figure, garbed in blue velvet trousers and jacket, appeared at the head of the stairs. It was as Vecchio had said.

Black, bottomless eyes peered from a mass of twisted pink and white flesh. There was no nose. Two dark, forbidding holes pierced the travesty of a face

above the curled scar-tissue of contorted lips. The chin receded, pulling down the lower lip and baring the wet surface of yellow-toothed gums.

A cry of horror escaped Jane's lips as the faceless figure came down the steps and approached. She cringed against Hugh, burying her head in the hollow of his shoulder.

Cagliostro paid her no attention. His brilliant eyes centered on Dr. Vecchio. When he was close enough, he nodded his head in greeting.

"You expected me, of course, Riccardo," Vecchio said softly.

Cagliostro's mouth quivered like wet worms. "Yes, but not tonight. I had heard that you were released." His eyes shifted to Jane and Hugh, lit up strangely.

"These are American friends of mine, Riccardo," Vecchio supplied. "We were traveling together on the Milan-Rome bus. A slight accident occurred. I told them you would grant them the comfort of your home until such time as passage to Rome can be secured."

What passed for a gracious smile twisted the mask of Cagliostro's face. "Of course! The pleasure is mine! You will remain with me until morning. Then I will have my car take you to Rome." He clapped his hands twice.

Hugh found voice. "That—that really isn't necessary," he said. "If you'll just permit me to telephone—"

"Nonsense!" He addressed the dwarf who had approached. "*Ubaldo! Prepara due stanze. Subito!*" He turned to Hugh. "I am arranging for a room for you and your wife. Am I correct?"

"I am sorry," Dr. Vecchio interjected. "*Signor e Signora* Bedford .... Dr. Riccardo Cagliostro, a former associate of mine."

Hugh acknowledged the introduction

nervously. He lifted Jane's head from his shoulder. "You'll have to excuse my wife," he explained. "The long trip and the accident—"

"Of course," Cagliostro murmured. "If you will follow me I will show you to your room."

HE LED the way up the stone steps and through a cavernous hall. As his fingers curled about the knob of a door, a muffled scream rang out. Jane's hands flew to her throat. Vecchio's eyes narrowed. But Dr. Cagliostro smiled faintly.

"It is nothing," he said. "We are experimenting with some animals in my laboratory. You hear the bleat of a lamb." He threw the door open.

"It—it sounded like a human voice," Jane gasped.

"A lamb, *signora*," he repeated slowly, facing Dr. Vecchio. "The adjoining room is yours, Giovanni." He bowed. "And now, I will bid you all *buona sera*."

In the privacy of the sumptuously furnished boudoir, Jane came into her husband's arms, every muscle in her slender body trembling.

"I'm afraid, Hugh," she panted. "He looks so—so horrible! It sends chills up and down my spine!"

His hands laved her curved body with reassuring strength, moving around her waist to cup the quivering mounds of her breasts. They caressed the resilient flesh, until the firm mounds quivered against his palm.

In the divine ecstasy of his touch, her fear dropped like a mantle. Parted lips met the offering of his mouth. Her hips arched trembling, against him. Body to body, they felt, as one person, the pounding of their hearts and the fervent beating of their pulses.

Hugh's fingers found the clasps of her blouse and soon the wet silk was being peeled from her upper body, baring magenta-peaked breasts under a thin, network brassiere. His lips had just slipped from her damp mouth when a knock at the door tensed both their bodies.

Jane grasped for her damp waist and held it over her young-breasted nudity. Hugh walked to the connecting door between their room and Dr. Vecchio's. He opened it slowly. Vecchio faced him, murmuring apologies.

"I should like to have a word with you, *Signor* Bedford," he whispered. Hugh stepped into the adjoining room. Vecchio closed the door to a crack. "I felt that I was duty bound to make you aware of my position here," he began. "In the first place, I have just been released from the *Porto Longone* prison where I served a three year sentence for a crime Dr. Cagliostro committed. I shall not bore you with the details, but let it suffice to say that we were joint discoverers of a serum which seemed to possess properties of injecting life into corpses."

He spoke hurriedly, as though in fear of imminent danger. "This serum, three years ago, was not yet perfected, and despite my warnings against its use, Dr. Cagliostro, forbidden by the authorities to obtain corpses, murdered a woman in order to attempt to bring her back to life. The fiendish crime was placed on my head, and through Cagliostro's false testimony, I was convicted. I have come back now to seek amends and also to discover the whereabouts of my wife and daughter, both of whom were brought under his evil spell after my incarceration."

HIS voice dropped to a shadow of its whisper. "I now see my mistake in bringing you and your charming bride to this house. Cagliostro has evidently gone mad in his search for the true secret of life after death. That cry you heard was a human cry, for beneath this

"You have told enough, Giovanni!"

A low, throaty voice filled the room. Vecchio wheeled as a panel slid back in the wall and Dr. Cagliostro stepped out of a black hole.

"You are young and your heart blood is fresh and clean," he told her.

house are the ancient catacombs of Rome, and it is in these hoary crypts, I suspect, that he takes life in a vain attempt to give it back again. I do not think he will bother either of you, *signor*, for his battle is only with me, but I have told you everything so that—"

"Too much, *mi amico*. In fact, enough to make this American very dangerous." His scarred mouth curled. "You have made it almost necessary for me to see to it that he never leaves this place again!'

Hugh was off his feet in a flying leap

before the last word had dripped from Cagliostro's lips. His muscled body hurtled through the air, striking the mad-man directly above the knees and sending him spinning into a corner. But, with the litheness and agility of a panther, Cagliostro ducked from under Hugh's clutching hands and came to his feet.

A steel-bladed knife flashed from beneath his velvet jacket. He took one step in the direction of the prostrate American and slashed down viciously.

At that moment Vecchio went into action. He was close to a dressing-table and his finger found a heavy hand-mirror. It sailed through the air end over end, smashing against the knife blade and spinning it from Cagliostro's hand.

The faceless scientist snarled and backed to the opening in the wall. He clapped his hands twice before Hugh beat him down with two terrifice smashes to the hideous hollow of his jaw.

AS HE fell, two giants of men dropped into the room from the wall hole. Hugh swung at the first one, but the blow glanced off the Goliath's ear. He heard a blood-curdling scream behind him, and turned just in time to see the dwarf, Ubaldo, leap up upon Jane's breasts and bear her to the ground. The outcry was his undoing.

The giant's mammoth fist crashed down on his skull with the impact of a sledge hammer. Again and again it beat his head until he staggered drunkenly from the cerebral shock. Through a haze he could see Jane on the floor, fighting off the clutching hands of the dwarf. Her brassiere had been ripped in two and hung from her shoulders, baring the heaving perfection of her alabaster breasts.

He stepped towards her, but his legs buckled under him as the pile-driving fist clipped the back of his neck. He dropped senseless.

CAGLIOSTRO, recovered from Hugh's blows, came to his feet. His face, ghastly in repose, was a nightmare in anger. He barked out orders curtly. One of the giants lifted Hugh's body in his arms, another raised the supine form of Jane. Ubaldo, the dwarf, kept Dr. Vecchio at bay with a blunt-nosed automatic, while they passed out of the room. Then, dismissing Ubaldo after relieving him of the gun, Cagliostro addressed his former associate.

"So, I am mad, am I?" His eyes sparked fire. "I am afraid, *mi amico*, it is you who are mad. You have been the cause of trouble which only silence can rectify—and silence is death!"

Vecchio's voice was singularly calm. "You dare not harm a hair of their heads, Riccardo! You will do well to release them both at once."

"I dare anything in the interest of science, *mi amico*." An insidious leer swept over his marred face. "The girl is young and will suit my purpose admirably. The boy I have no use for, but he knows too much. As for you, none will believe the story of a convicted murderer!"

Vecchio started, but the gun in Cagliostri's hand swayed menacingly. "Stand back, Giovanni," he warned. "I am taking no further chances. There is too much at stake. Much has happened in the three years you have been away. Soon . . . any day now, I will have the secret of life after death in my hands. At this very moment—"

Again a muffled human scream echoed eerily. Vecchio turned white. "Where is my wife, Lucia, and my daughter, Bianca?" he demanded.

Cagliostro's eyes gave birth to a distant opaqueness. "Lucia sleeps," he murmured.

"You will awaken her and tell her I am here!"

"Awaken her?" The repetition was distantly ephemeral. "No, not yet. When the time comes she will rise from her couch like a naked Venus. Until then, she must sleep."

The cords of Vecchio's neck twanged taut. "Murderer!" he screamed. "You've killed Lucia!"

"Killed? No, Giovanni, the Venus is not dead. She sleeps until the power of my genius will arouse her." He stepped to the door. "Come, I will show you." Still brandishing the automatic, he led the way down a rear flight of steps, through a heavy steel door and into the damp muskiness of the underground catacombs.

Oil lamps, suspended from the arched stone ceilings, pierced the cold gloom with flickering yellow light. On either side of the long galleries, crude markings on the walls indicated the burial places of Rome's ancient dead.

A T THE end of one corridor, Cagliostro pulled an iron ring projecting from the wall. A stone door slid back slowly, Vecchio followed him into a large room. On raised platforms, glass sepulchers enclosed the naked bodies of women. Cagliostro approached one.

"Here," he whispered, "Lucia sleeps!"

Like a man in a trance, Vecchio moved to the glass-covered couch. The nude, white loveliness of his wife was stretched out before him. Her flesh was alabaster pale, the breasts rising like conical mounds of snow. They were still, void of the breath of life, but the curved sweep of limb, clean and velvet-smoth, seemed to be resting in peaceful repose. Her hair, a cascade of silken ebony, fell about her shoulders, tendrils of it framing the quiet breasts.

Vecchio stood silently by the sepulcher. Then, suddenly he sprang at Cagliostro, taloned hands reaching for the mad scientist's throat. A booming shout broke the stillness of the death vault. The lead pellet burned through Vecchio's arm, spinning him around like a top. Unmindful of the hot stab of pain, he came at Cagliostro again, clinching with him just as the automatic barked for the second time.

"Killer!" he screamed, slashing at the hideous face. The gun twirled in Cagliostro's hand. He stepped back, swung his arm, and brought the butt crashing down on Vecchio's skull. The physician moaned softly and crumpled to the stone floor.

A moment later the dwarf, Ubaldo, was at his master's side.

"You have taken care of the two?" Cagliostro questioned.

"Si, padrone."

"Buono!" He pointed to the prone figure of Dr. Vecchio. "See that he is made comfortable in his chamber." He paused at the glass crypt of Lucia Vecchio and touched the spot above her lips reverently. Then, without a word, he left the vault.

H UGH BEDFORD cracked heavy eye-lids to look up into the horribly gnarled features of Dr. Cagliostro.

"I offer my apologies, signore," the scientist said, "for your having made it necessary to cause you physical discomfort. Unfortunately, too, the poor tact of your friend, Dr. Vecchio, has placed you in a delicate position. I wish you to understand that I have no desire to do you personal harm, but under the conditions, it will be essential that you remain in this establishment until such time as I may see fit to release you. I warn you, there is no escape. To attempt it will mean to die!" He strode to the door.

Hugh strained at the hempen bonds that held him to the couch. "My wife!" he screamed. "Where is my wife?"

Cagliostro faced him. *"La signora* is in good hands," he replied, fading from the room.

A mute moan of terror greeted the scientist as he entered the chamber where Jane was held a prisoner. He turned the key in the lock as she cringed in the corner, striving desperately to shield the nudity of her breasts, and at the same time mask her eyes to his obnoxious ugliness.

Unperturbed, Cagliostro advanced to the center of the room. *"Vi chieggo perdone, signora.* The hands of my servant were no doubt rough and coarse upon your fair skin." He bowed low. "It shall not happen again."

Jane found voice. "Let me out of here!" she screamed. "You're a fiend!"

"I am neither a fiend, *signora,* nor a mad-man, as our mutual friend, Dr. Vecchio, would have you believe. I am, admittedly, entranced by your signal beauty and youth." He came towards her slowly. "If you will believe that I intend doing you no harm, all will be well. With your help I may be able to solve the secret of physical rejuvenation. The others have all been older. You are young and your heart-blood is fresh and clean." He rubbed his hands together sensually. The black holes of his eyes shot erotic fire.

Jane went white. "No! No! Don't touch me!"

"It is nothing," he murmured. "You will sleep just as my Venus and the others are sleeping, only your slumber will not be so long. I shall give you a new life!"

"No! No! Oh, God!"

His mouth curled. "Then your husband, *signora,* will die! It is one or the other. You have your choice."

She dropped to her knees. "Please! For the love of mercy! Don't kill him!"

"Then——?" He licked the shapeless scars of his lips with a flat, serrated tongue.

"Yes, I will do anything . . . . anything!" she gasped.

He was beside her in an instant, lifting her from the floor. Jane went sick with revulsion as the twisted slime of his mouth covered her lips. She closed her eyes, praying for insensibility to blanket the horror of his tenuous fingers laving the smooth solidity of her breasts. It came, but not soon enough.

Her exhausted body screamed out in agony to the harsh intimacy of his caresses. She was too weak, too tired and too sick to fight him off. If only Hugh were saved, nothing mattered.

Nothing . . . nothing . . . nothing . . .

THE skin of his arms torn and lacerated by the ropes that bound him, Hugh Bedford relaxed on the couch, resigned to whatever might come. His only thoughts were of Jane and her safety. If Cagliostro—!

The hall door opened slowly and a young girl came into the room. Her dark eyes blinked curiously at Hugh and she hesitated before crossing the threshold. She was clothed in a cotton nightdress, little protection for the slim nubility of her childish breasts and delicately arched hips.

"I am sorry," she said softly, "but I heard a woman's voice and I thought

"Your father—"

"My father is dead, *signore*," she said, "and my mother afflicted with a strange malady. Dr. Cagliostro is ministering to her." Her eyes softened. "I pray each night to the Blessed Theresa for her well-being."

In his right hand he held a hypodermic syringe, its needle pointing at her bosom.

possibly *mia madre* had awakened." She curtsied with naive grace. "I am Bianca."

"Bianca!" Hugh echoed the name. He remembered what Dr. Vecchio had told him. So this was his daughter. Bianca!

In a flash, the whole diabolical scheme of things became clear. As Hugh gave rapid instructions, Bianca removed a penknife from his pocket and cut the bonds. Free, he raced through the upper hall, calling out Dr. Vecchio's name. There was a muffled answer from a locked room. In three lunges the door crashed in.

Hugh ripped the gag and ropes from the physician and lifted him to his feet. Together they searched each room for Jane, but fruitlessly. Finally, Vecchio led the way to the steel catacomb door.

Perspiration, cold and clammy, broke out of Hugh's face as he followed Vecchio into the underground tombs. The graves built into the walls had crumbled before the ravages of time, and here a white, shiny skull protruded, there the gaunt skeleton of a leg.

At the vault door, Vecchio motioned for silence. He was about to pull the iron ring which would swing back the stone block, when the scrape of feet sounded behind them. They turned together, in time to see Ubaldo, the dwarf, leap at them with two stilettos, one clutched in each hand.

Hugh sidestepped, drawing Vecchio with him. The dwarf hurtled through the air, his head crashing up against the jagged granite. There was a dull *pop,* like the cracking of a melon, and Ubaldo's skull split in two. He dropped like a plummet into a welter of gushing blood, the vicious knives clattering to the floor.

FOOTSTEPS pounded in the vaulted corridor. Through the haze, Vecchio saw the twin giants bearing down on them. He stooped quickly and lifted the stilettos. As the mammoth men came within range, the knives left his whipped hand point first, lodging, with deadly accuracy, to the left of each sternum, buried to the hilts above the men's hearts. Before their bodies had dropped, Vecchio pulled the iron ring.

The stone door swung back. Hugh gaped at the sight that met his eyes. Under a powerful carbon light, Dr. Cagliostro, garbed in white from head to foot, was bending over the naked body of Jane. His left hand cupped her breast, lifting it gently. In his right he held a hypodermic syringe, its needle point moving to a spot below her white bosom.

"Stop!"

Vecchio's voice rang out and boomed through the vault. Cagliostro turned suddenly. The carbon light threw a green cast over his mad face, hollowing the pits of his eyes.

Vecchio's command roused Hugh from his terrified trance. He leaped across the room. Cagliostro screamed out an insane curse. The hypo flashed and he buried it needle-deep into his arm, jamming down on the plunger. In an instant the maniac's body shook with convulsions and his face turned blue. He gasped for breath, sinking to his knees and clutching at his throat.

Before Dr. Vecchio could reach him, he was on his back, dead! The physician picked up the hypo and smelled the tip.

"Prussic acid," he said quietly.

Hugh had Jane in his arms. "Yes, she's alive!" he gasped. "And—and so is your daughter, Bianca! I left her upstairs!"

Hours later, as they drove towards Rome, bearing the body of Lucia, Dr. Vecchio hurled the ashes of the incompleted rejuvenation formula to the night winds.

"There will be life and there will be death," he said softly, "but man may tamper with neither."

THE ISLE OF THE RESTLESS DEAD

[Continued from page 27]

out his revolver and fired. In the confines of the cathedral, the report was deafening. He strode behind the altar, revolver ready.

"So that's it! Hands up, McAndrew! You beat me to it for once—but not for long! Come out of there—you hard-boiled islander! Got you this time!"

There was nothing but to obey. The crowd of brown men had surged into

The jerk nearly tore his arm from its socket, but he held on to her desperately.

the door, drawn by the report. With malicious triumph, Mayo beckoned them on.

"Get rope, you fella. Tie him up—good!" He prodded McAndrew in the stomach with the muzzle of his revolver.

THEY did the job thoroughly and expeditiously, those Kanaka seamen. Malaita men, most of them, sinister and evil-faced. Men who had tasted long-pig—who had ground baked human flesh between those filed teeth and smacked their thick lips over it. Only one held back, a scarred, bearded warrior, naked save for his scarlet *pareu*. His eyes rolled ghastly whites. Through his thick lips he muttered incessantly, *"Akua-akua! Akua-akua!"*

"He'll be a departed spirit, damn' quick!" snarled Mayo. "Listen, Mac, what about those pearls? Don't tell me you haven't found them!"

"They're where you'll never lay your paws on them!" McAndrew snapped.

"I can find ways to make you talk!" He beat the prisoner savagely over the head with his clubbed revolver, until the blood ran over his lacerated face.

Mayo strode over to the girl's defiant figure. "Feel like loosening up?"

"No, damn you!" McAndrew grated.

With one swift movement Mayo caught the girl's thin costume. He ripped it from neck to waistline, tore the garment from her shoulders. His hands played gloatingly over the soft curves of the girl's figure, over the white flesh, hidden only by her scanty undergarments.

"First I'll have my fun with this *vahine* of yours, then—well, after I'm through and my men have her—" he leered at the evil faces of the Malaita men who crowded around, licking their sensuous lips.

McAndrew groaned helplessly. "You've got me! If I tell you where they are—will you let her go?"

"Not making any promises, Mac. But if you don't tell—you know what she'll get—"

"I didn't think a man who calls himself white could be quite so rotten! Look behind that altar, damn you!"

Mayo bent and retrieved the casket. He flung the top open, poured the iridescent globules through his fingers in a glittering stream. An insane light flared in his eyes.

"Rich—rich for life!" he panted. "I can leave these damn' islands—Paris—London—Monte Carlo—God, what can't a man do with a fortune like this!"

He strode over lustfully toward Velma. "Thanks for the tip, Mac. Saved me a little trouble. Just for that I won't shoot you—just leave you on that damned altar to starve—and while the crabs are picking your bones, I'll be sailing away with the *vahine*—and the treasure—"

He tore gloatingly at the girl's scant garments. The narrow brassiere broke, her full, unrestrained breasts quivered helplessly under his clawing fingers. His hand swept to the yoke at her waist, tore at the thin silk.

McAndrew, bound and helpless, surged at him in impotent rage.

The bearded Kanaka, eyes still wide with terror at this reincarnation of his supposedly dead captain, had crept to the profaned altar. He caught up the fallen cross, lifted it high—

MAYO whirled suddenly, sensing something wrong. He fired, once, twice, at short range. The bullets tore through the gigantic Kanaka's shoulder, through his chest. But even as the

The ghostly form took shape beside her. "Dick! Dick!" she cried.

brown man staggered, crimson blood spurting over the dark skin, the great cross descended with all his strength in a crushing blow.

Mayo gurgled, fired once more, as his fingers tightened convulsively at the trigger. He fell limp and spreadeagled, clutching at the nacre of the altar. The cross crashed into a hundred fragments over him.

The native clutched desperately at his wounds, and staggered to the bound figure of his captain. He whipped his knife from his loin cloth, he slashed convulsively at the ropes. As the cords fell away, he sank on one knee, fingers dyed red from the blood that was welling from his chest and shoulder.

McAndrew surged to his feet. The little group of natives had for the moment fallen back. They rushed in, barbed spears lifted.

McAndrew stooped swiftly, caught at the revolver that had clattered upon the foot of the altar. He fired twice at the onrushing pack. One huge savage went down gurgling with a bloody froth on his lips. Another bearded cannibal flung his spear and dropped with a bullet through his heart.

The spear clattered and smashed on the iridescent shell of the altar. The

His knee rose desperately. With a savage grunt Mayo relaxed his clamp for a split-second. McAndrew writhed, wrenched himself free, caught his tormentor with one desperate burst of strength. A cunning wrestler's hold—he swung the pirate clear of the ground, spun him in a whirling circle, and flung him toward the ruined altar.

Flesh and blood could not withstand that maddened lunge. Mayo thudded sickeningly upon the hard nacre. The

---

Look for these stories next month—

MASTER OF DEATH   BLOOD DRINKERS

PHANTOM OF FAIRMOUNT

GODDESS OF TERROR   EYES OF MALTHA

Reserve your copy now!

September issue on sale July 15th

---

others scuffed backward, and fled with wild cries from that bloody shambles.

Mayo struggled to his knees, cleared his reeling brain, then charged in with a bellowing roar only a shade less hideous than those of his crew. McAndrew's lips tightened as he pressed the trigger.

The hammer snapped on an empty cylinder.

With an insane roar Mayo charged. His lean hands closed about McAndrew's throat. Cramped, half-starved, numb from the cruel blows that Mayo had rained upon him as lay trussed, the captain felt himself bent backward. The shell-lined walls swam before his gaze.

altar reeled at the impact. The pirate leader lay inert, neck broken, hands gripping at the polished pearl-shell.

And over the two combatants, one reeling and breathless, the other dead as the long-departed native chiefs, stood an all but naked girl, grasping defiantly the reddened knife that she had caught from the hand of the blood-smeared Karoni, prepared to fight off the rush of the bronze natives.

But no rush came. With howls of fear the dark-hued Kanakas had fled. After all, they had no love for Mayo's kicks and curses—and the *akua-akuas* were very powerful.

THE phosporescent waves lapped idly at the *Ghost's* sides as the schooner slipped once more through the tropic seas, Tahiti-bound. Motu Akua and its restless dead lay a faint blur on the horizion. On the aft deck two figures leaned against the moonlit rail.

Dick McAndrew slipped his arm about Velma's slender waist.

"Double quantity of treasure on board," he grinned. "Pearls worth an emperor's ransom in the cabin—and out here—"

Her head dropped on his shoulder. The haunting moonlight silvered her hair, the patched sails of the schooner, the prosphorescent wake behind.

Her face was upturned, just below his lips that sought to descend upon hers. Her arms tightened about his bronzed neck, her lips parted—

"I've found more than treasure out here in the Islands," she murmured so softly that the words barely reached his ears. "I've found—the man—I dreamed of—"

MATE FOR MEDUSA

[Continued from page 43]

"Believe me, Mr. Martin, I was more than delighted with your appearance here this evening! I might even call you the answer to my prayer! For a long time I have needed a patient possessing both brain and muscle for one of my little experiments. You should be very happy, Martin, very happy, for the opportunity to father a race of giants! Think of it! The honor! The glory!

"Many things I have accomplished in a busy life. I have learned to graft complete limbs so that they are usable. I have evolved snakes with feet, lizards with wings! But tonight, I hope, marks the culmination of my career! For I, Leo Lombard, am finished with guinea pigs and white rats! Tonight I use humans as subjects!"

The woman stirred beside Martin. In spite of himself he turned and looked, blood coursing madly through his veins at sight of her unadorned loveliness. The doctor laughed.

"Do not look at the woman yet, Mar-

tin! And do not be alarmed at what you feel! I have just given you the most powerful stimulant ever devised, in order that you may play your part tonight. But not with this woman! You are going to father a race of giants! Wait for me, and while you wait think of the women you have known.

"Women, Martin, with lovely, white bodies soft to touch; women sighing in sudden passion; women breathing deep in the stress of emotion. Shortly I shall bring you your wife for tonight, the mother of the race of giants which I, Lombard, shall give the world!"

He pattered from the room. Martin lay silent, trying to make sense of the whole thing, trying to keep down the torturing thoughts that filled his mind. In spite of those efforts the predominating thought was of the white form beside him. Like a lodestone her lovely body drew him. He surrendered to an impulse stronger than his will, turning to drink her beauty.

Rhythmically those generous breasts rose and fell. Breath rippled down across her flat stomach. He caressed her a thousand times with burning eyes. His conscious mind told him it was the hypodermic at work, yet he could not fight off the effects.

He yearned for this woman, so gleaming and white beside him, yearned for her with a passionate intensity he had never before experienced. Only the sound of the opening door prevented him from rolling ruthlessly, recklessly, toward her.

LOMBARD stepped into the room leading a woman, or a caricature of a woman, as one leads a bashful child. The negro, Harry, giggled; Martin gasped in astonishment. The woman who paddled so meekly behind the misshapen doctor was fully eight feet tall and built in proportion. She simpered, mincing along, dwarfing her companion. Her features, nearly double normalcy, plainly bore a resemblance to those of Helen Vinton!

"Quiet, Mona," the doctor said, pausing beside the table. "Quiet, dearest! Let me put this little needle into your arm to help you, and then you shall have a nice husband!"

He roared with laughter at his horrible joke, as Martin stiffened convulsively on the bed. Lombard injected the drug into the woman's elephantine arm.

"You see," he explained gravely, "this is Mona, my wife, the sister of the woman on the bed beside you. If I am willing to sacrifice her to the good of future humanity in the production of a race of giants surely you will not refuse to aid!" He roared with laughter again.

"As a matter of fact you won't be able to refuse! Until you dropped in as a gift from the gods I was more or less at a loss as to my next step. By operating on the pituitary gland of little Mona I have enlarged her body to tremendous dimensions, but alas, it has affected her mind!

"Of course that, as well as her size, can be remedied by another operation, but I trust the children of the union will inherit muscle and brain power from their father, Mr. Martin," he bowed ironically, "and stature from their mother, who was once my well loved wife!"

At a word of instruction the negro lifted Martin from the bed, carried him across the room to lay him on the floor. The doctor laid the huge woman there beside him. "Now," he laughed, "simply lie still, and shortly you shall be released, my fortunate friend!"

The enormous mounds of her breasts rose and fell beside Martin. Repulsive, nauseating as they were he could not keep his eyes from them. She smiled down into his face with the vacuous questioning grin of an idiotic child. Her huge paw of a hand reached forth to caress his face, and when he turned aside, she thrust a bulky arm beneath his neck, across his shoulder, big fingers sliding down beneath his shirt.

The touch of her palm was moist and hot on his bare flesh; her breath was quick and passionate. In spite of his loathing his own blood flared hotly. Then his eye caught sight of the negro walking on tiptoe, bearing something out of the door.

It was the nude form of the unconscious Helen Vinton.

"Look!" gasped Martin, and the intent Lombard turned. The negro stopped at the doctor's word of command. He laid the white figure on the floor, turned to meet his advancing master.

A relentless hand closed about his throat. Martin strained to the utmost.

stretched. Only fumbling movement in his breast hinted at the third dangerous appendage nestling there.

The woman behind him breathed heavily, sighed, clasped Martin to her tremendous bosom. Great, gross breasts pulsed and vibrated against him. A heavy leg pinned him to the floor and blood coursed hotter and hotter through his veins. Across her shoulder he saw Clauser shake his head like a mastiff, stumble to his knees.

A SHOT shattered the pregnant silence of the room. The negro sank slowly to the floor, clutching at his throat. The gun was held in the doctor's third hand. Something glinted on the middle finger as he tossed the gun contemptuously at the dying negro, glinted and flashed even more as he picked up

"She's mine, mine, I tell you!" the negro rumbled. His white third arm crept out of the slotted blouse; steel gleamed in the lamplight. The doctor advanced slowly, his own arms out-the inert body of the fallen woman and bore her white loveliness to the bed.

Only Martin heard the gibbering, driving mutterings of the armless one in the corner.

"My ring! My hand! He's got my hand!" The words were low. There was madness on Clauser's contorted features.

Lombard turned from the bed, walked toward Martin. He licked his thin lips, eyes yet burning insanely.

"Plenty of time for that later," he leered at Martin. "Now, my very good friend, if my drug is successful, and I believe it is, we'll go on with our little experiment."

He leaned over, fumbled at the bonds on Martin's wrists. Behind him Martin saw the silent, creeping approach of the armless one, the ex-reporter, Clauser. He prayed that his hands would be freed before the madman charged. As the last knot gave Clauser launched himself, feet foremost, like a wrestler.

"Thief! Thief!" he gibbered. "Give me my arm!"

Lombard was overborne. One sinewy leg spanned his thick throat; the other crossed over it on the right side to hook tenaciously beneath his armpit. Together they rolled, pitched, tumbled on the floor, that sinewy leg grinding deeper and deeper into the windpipe it pressed so relentlessly. The madman shrieked and gibbered as three hands tore at his flesh, but Martin was too engrossed in his own struggle to lend aid.

THE woman, Mona, twined huge arms about his body, pressing him closer and closer, literally smothering him in her passionate embrace. It required a busy three minutes to break loose.

When he finally arose Clauser sat panting in a corner, his bony heels beating a terrible tattoo on the bloody mass that once had been Lombard's face. It took another ten minutes to quiet the armless one.

A half hour later the city desk of the *News* received a call from its best feature writer, Eddie Martin.

From the dead doctor's telephone Martin disclosed parts of his amazing story, pausing only once—long enough to turn to a woman who sobbed over the eight foot figure of her sister.

"Don't cry, sweetheart," he murmured. "Lombard himself said she could be restored to normalcy by another operation. Surely somewhere in the world is a doctor that knows how to do it! We'll find him, find him together! You and I! Together from now on!"

HELL HOLE OF HORROR

[Continued from page 75]

full breast brushed against his shoulder. Now he knew it was no fanciful dream.

"Are you all right?" she gasped.

He wanted her to touch him again. More than anything, he wanted the warm softness of her against him, the clinging moisture of her poppy mouth.

Only that would convince him he was in a world of reality, and not consorting with phantasms of a spectral sphere.

"Yes .... I'm all right." He reached up and touched his fingers to the soft breasts above him. She drew away, not in fright, but with an unknowing innocence.

desire. It was excruciating pain to lift himself up beside her, but it was pain that would have its reward.

His right arm circled her waist, the questing hand coming up under a full breast, lifting it until the white flesh

He fought back with the mad fury of one who has seen the bottomless pit of death.

Lane understood. "Please," he whispered. "Please let me hold you."

She hesitated, but Lane found her hand and drew her down. Only then did he realize he was no longer in the Black Forest, but in the bare room of a log cabin, stretched on a cot. But even that failed to divert him.

The curve of the girl's thigh burned his skin, the body-warmth of her lush figure sent him into ecstasies of poignant bulged from her bodice. Her soft, panting breath fanned Lane's cheek. The fingers of his free hand found her bosom. Pushing aside the protecting cloth with rough eagerness, his hand touched globular, velvet smoothness, pressed its yielding warmth. Lane's mouth searched out the writhing flame of her lips. It was paradise . . . too keen . . . too ecstatically perfect.

BLISSFUL minutes later her low voice brought him out of the peaceful inertia into which he had willingly slipped.

"You must go!" she breathed. "If she should see you here—"

The horror that had gone before this heaven on earth came back to Lane. All his senses revolted against it, bringing before him the mission on which he had come.

"Who do you mean?" he questioned.

Whispered fear marked her reply. "La Belle! She will set the snakes on you! It is long past dawn. Go! I beg you!"

Taut terror crept into Lane's voice. "You mean—you mean the creature of the forest?" he gasped. "The thing that attacked me?"

"No, but he is La Belle's, too. I drove him off in the forest, but he will return. He belongs to La Belle. She made him from one of the babies. The rest, more twisted even, were sold to circuses. It is a mania with her. She is mad!"

As the ghastly canvas unfolded, Lane's skin crawled as though it were infested with maggots. *A curse!* Willoughby had almost been right! In this unexplored fastness was a ghoul who twisted the bodies of infants to make freaks for a circus! *Circus!* The word rang uncannily. Colonel Matt Elkins, the millionaire circus owner! La Belle! Did it all mean something? He held the girl's cold hands.

"And who are you?" Each word

seared his lips. He was afraid of the answer.

"My name is Elsa," she said softly. "La Belle says that my father was a great man and—and—"

Lane stiffened. "And *what?*"

Shame pinked her cheeks. "And that *she* is my *mother!*" Her breath quickened. "But it cannot be! La Belle is a witch. She keeps snakes—hundreds of them—in baskets! Each has a gold chain on its tail. It was one that had escaped that you killed! I was sent to find it! I—"

A rasping cackle sounded above Elsa's strained, gasping voice. "La Belle!" she panted. "Oh, God!"

THE door creaked open slowly. Lane's eyes followed the widening crack. An emaciated hand slithered along the jamb, followed by a thin arm and then the most depraved feminine face the human mind could imagine.

Matted gray hair hung in filthy disorder over hollowed cheeks, sucked so far in as to push the bones almost through the gray, wrinkled skin. The crone had no teeth, and as she leered, pink gums drooled a bubbly saliva.

Elsa screamed and fell back against the wall in chilled terror. Lane came off the cot, facing the hideous, foul-faced hag. As though her ugliness were not enough, the creature of the Black Forest, his malformed head more gruesome by daylight, crawled into the cottage behind his mistress.

Lane noted the wicker basket hanging from the crone's right arm. He remembered what Elsa had said about snakes in baskets. It was their only chance! Either death for all of them, or—?

La Belle's cracked voice sounded.

"Thought you'd rob me, eh?" she cackled. "Thought I didn't know, eh?" Her cadaverous hand patted the basket. "These'll fix yuh fer meddlin'. Heh! Heh! Heh! These'll fix yer!"

Lane dropped back to where Elsa cringed against the wall. His left arm circled her waist. "Don't worry," he whispered. "Just relax."

Slowly, he led her towards the hag and her horrible creature. La Belle screamed out a warning, fumbled with the cover of the basket. Releasing Elsa, Lane leaped forward, swung one foot in a football kick and caught the basket with the toe of his shoe. It spun through the air, crashed against the wall and split apart. Rattlesnakes—slimy coils of them—slithered to the floor.

Lane struck the hag across the face, knocked her down. The malformed creature bolted for the open door, but a driving fist caught him under the chin and dropped him. All in a split second, Lane whirled, lifted Elsa in his arms and lunged for safety.

A snake struck just as he thundered through the door, missing Elsa's leg by a hair's-breadth.

Outside, Lane dropped his precious burden. Before even one of the reptiles could escape the hut, he had the door closed and was holding it. La Belle's shrieks of terror were blood-curdling. The rattling of the diamond-backs, like the angry whipping of a thousand dry leaves, was a ghastly obligato.

Lane could see them striking again and again, perforating the ghoul's flesh with their sharp fangs. The shrieks became hysterical words.

"Not good enough fer you, Matt Elkins, am I?" La Belle screamed. "Well, I fixed yer! Stole her away from yuh and brought her up as mine! And

the rest! Heh! Heh! To the circus, Matt! Where you found me! Freaks, that's what I made out of them! *Freaks!* Every one of 'em but yours. Her I brought up like she was mine because she should have been!" The voice died out in a groan. There was silence within the hut.

Elsa was weeping softly. "The last baby . . . . it's in the other house," she murmured.

Lane folded her in his arms. "Don't cry, darling. You have everything to live for now. It's all over . . . . and I love you!"

Their mouths met and clung.

THE EXECUTIONER

[Continued from page 15]

coping of the roof, hesitated, poised his body. He stared below.

The scene was strange to him; he did not recognize it. There was no courtyard; no headsman's block. Kathy's headless body wasn't there. Von Kemmerer's corpse had vanished. Instead, Gerard looked down upon a steady procession of traffic—taxicabs, street-cars, trucks.

"New York!" he gasped. And he launched himself forward off the roof, into eternity.

————

From the New York *Bulletin,* March 21st, 1935:

HOSPITAL PATIENT
    LEAPS FROM ROOF;
        TAKES OWN LIFE

William Gerard, 31, New York advertising man, leaped from the roof of St. George's Hospital to his death late yes-terday afternoon, while temporarily deranged. He had been the victim of an automobile accident two weeks ago, at which time he suffered concussion of the brain. It is thought that his suicide was due to delirium.

By an old coincidence, Gerard's twin brother, Erich Gerhardt, committed suicide in Berlin at practically the same hour of the same day, according to cabled despatches. The brothers had been separated in childhood, and had not seen one another in twenty-five years.

Gerhardt, the German twin, was a Nazi executioner whose headsman's axe had brought death to scores of anti-Hitler sympathizers. He had just executed a woman accused of espionage, and immediately thereafter ran amuck, killing Graf von Kemmerer, a government official, with his axe.

He then ran to the roof of the prison building and threw himself to his death on the courtyard below, at precisely the same time his brother in New York was taking his life under identical circumstances.

What One Reader Says!

(And this is only a single instance of an unsolicited reaction that may honestly be called nation-wide!)

Gentlemen:

At last—a He-man's magazine in America! Let me salute this first real gleam of the coming sunrise of masculinity after the long night of feminist decadence in a once virile land!

Hail to you! gentlemen, and to Spicy-Adventure Stories. And do not falter in this glorious come-back of red-blooded fiction in a country gone effete.

We need the reawakening of the HE-MAN in America. The psychology of your magazine is masculine. It will help.

Sincerely yours,

For a long time the publishers of Spicy-Adventure Stories had felt the keenness of the need for a magazine, alive, vital, packed with red corpuscles. That is how Spicy-Adventure Stories was born.

And now you may judge for yourselves

SPICY - ADVENTURE STORIES

August issue—on sale everywhere—July 2nd

NAGA'S KISS

[Continued from page 55]

"Kill me if you wish, master," said Shir Singh. "I killed the *Nagâ* woman to save you from evil. I got a weapon from the King of Wizards—a weapon of explosives and magic—"

Finlay's face was white, but his brain

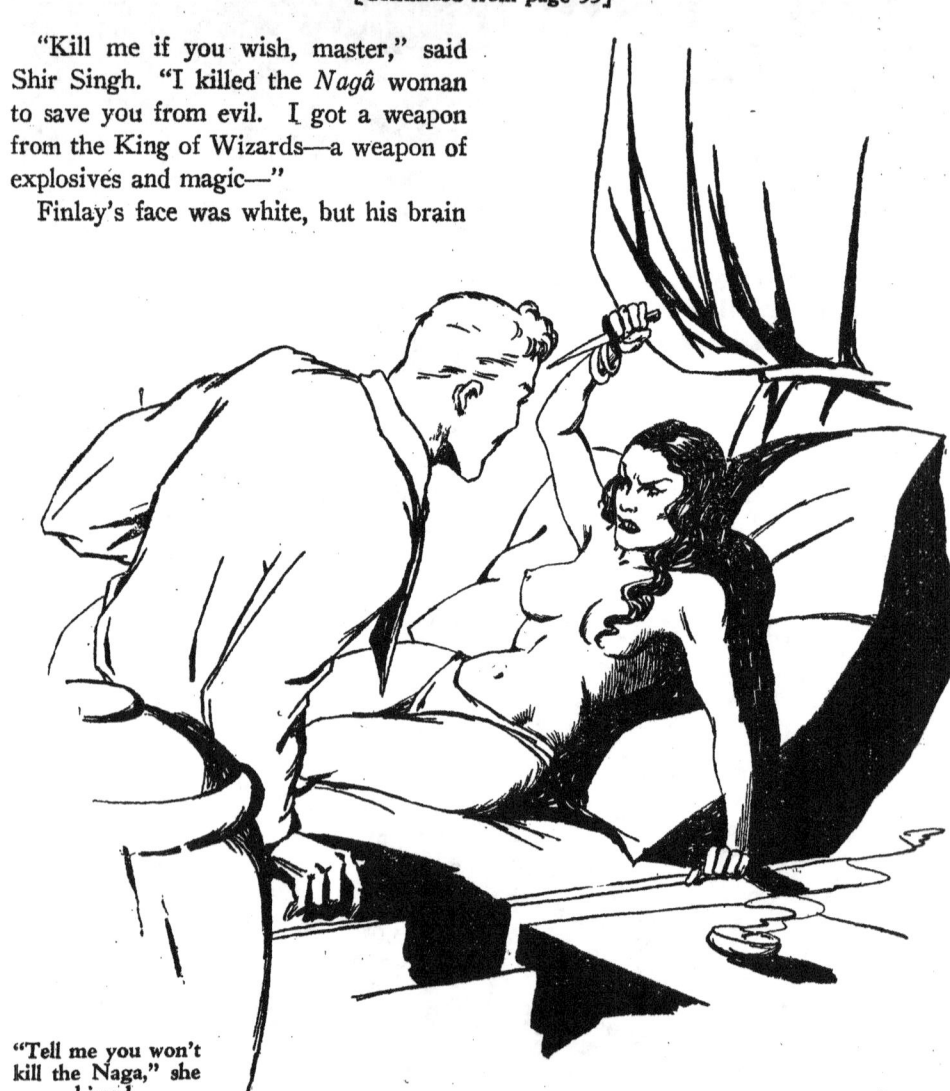

"Tell me you won't kill the Naga," she hissed.

was a red confusion. The rifle slowly rose into line. Then he remembered how that bearded giant had faced the monstrous apparition. That was more than valor.

"God damn you, Shir Singh!" Finlay

muttered bitterly. "I didn't want to be saved. . . ."

He flung the rifle into the underbrush.

"You're heavier'n hell, you big ox, but maybe I can get you back to camp."

And without looking back at the hideous remains of shattered loveliness, Finlay shouldered his servant, and headed for the *dâk* bungalow.

OUT OF THE TOMB

[Continued from page 87]

staggered backward, and in the eerie light Martin saw a tall man draped in black.

With a hoarse grunt of fighting joy he dove forward. sent a furious welter of blows into that sinister black figure.

The Black One, stumbling, gasping, fought back with the savagery of a cornered rat; sent hard, flying fists again and again to Martin's face; sliced his lips, brought a frothy rush of blood from his nose. But Martin bored in like a juggernaut; silent, inexorable, smashing home blows with terrible force.

The Black One caught a driving right full on his draped chin. It hurtled him against the stone wall and before he could recover Martin was upon him; had ripped away the black hood. Unmasked, the blackmailer dived for the door, fumbled with the heavy iron handles and had swung it partly open before Martin reached him, dragged him around.

JUST for a moment a blinding streak of lightning stabbed the darkness, brilliantly lighted the tiny barred window. Martin gasped, stepped back in amazement. He was staring into the dark, Spanish features of Ramos Costigo!

The latter took full advantage of Martin's momentary daze. He lashed out a straight hard blow that whacked viciously on Martin's chin, sent him to the floor. In almost the same motion he had torn the vault door open.

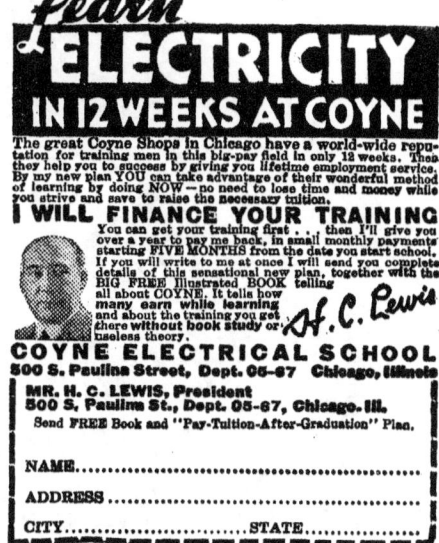

"You've suffered enough," he said. "I'm going to take you away."

For an instant his tall, draped figure was silhouetted in the doorway and in that instant a streak of livid flame belched from the blackness of the tomb, coupled itself with the thunderous roar of a gun.

Ramos Costigo whirled, tottered and crashed forward on his face.

Dazed, Martin came to his feet, struck a match. He leaned over Costigo, examined him hastily, found him quite dead. Turning, the flare of the match fell on the nude legs of Helen Stone and, standing by the trap door, her white-faced father, w i t h Costigo's smoking revolver in his hand. The dope-glazed eyes of the old man were blank, expressionless. His face was that of a

The Name Tells The Story!

Not just another detective story magazine!

SUPER - Detective Stories

And it's just what the title implies

It's bigger in size—

It has more illustrations, and they are printed in rotogravure—

It contains faster-moving, better worked-out stories.

It's a magazine that no detective-story fan can afford to miss, written by the best writers, put out in a more attractive form.

Ask for Super-Detective Stories

July issue now on sale at all newsstands

hynotized man who has no realization of what he has done.

"I came through the tunnel," Andrew Stone mumbled. His vóice was thick and he spoke into distance, vaguely, uncertainly. "I heard noises. I climbed up here. A gun was lying on the floor. I picked it up. I saw him go out the door. I shot him. I had to."

"Hasheesh!" Martin murmured to the stunned girl. "He doesn't know what he's done. Costigo fed it to him and because of it, your father's killed him."

HELEN STONE had reached a breaking point. Sobbing, she flung her arms about her dazed father. Martin strode to the doorway, gazed down on the body of Costigo, tried to collect his scattered thoughts.

"Vampires!" he mused. "He fed me that tale on the way up here, hoping it would frighten me off. When it didn't he slipped away, unlocked the vault door and put on that black robe he must have kept here. Then he bashed me on the head—figured when I came to he'd be far away before I could find any way to get this tomb open. . . ."

Shakily he lit a cigarette, stared at the storm-torn night. The reporter in him rose to the surface; his blue eyes were far away, seeing headlines:

"Girl lured to cemetery," he muttered aloud, "by rich playboy. Father follows, is attacked by seducer; kills him in self defense!"

"But—" came the quavering voice of the old man. "It wasn't that way at all. I—"

"It's got to be that way!" Martin interrupted firmly. "Don't you see? For her sake—for your sake! You've suffered enough!"

Martin lifted Helen Stone in his arms. through the thin raincoat he had placed on her, the warm, vibrant pressure of her thighs came as grateful balm. Her arms encircled his neck suddenly; her breasts flattened themselves on his chest.

In the warm brush of her lips across his cheek there was a glowing promise. "Come on," he said.

"Where?"

"Anywhere—away from here. Another city—another state—what does it matter—as long as we get your father away and cure him!"

Thunder rolled from the black heavens; cold rain swept over empty sodden fields as they left the vault. In the jagged flashes of lightning they saw the lonely, sweep of Bayhead Island revealed, desolate and grim.

They climbed in Andrew Stone's car and drove away.

DEAD LEGS WALK

[Continued from page 67]

And as Dexter fought to free himself, he saw the *legs* moving slowly, weirdly, impossibly, toward the bed. . . . Saw them *walking,* although they were disembodied, amputated. . . .

"You damn fiend!" he shouted insanely. And with a tremendous effort,

he released himself from Doris Killian's arms; sprang to his feet; launched himself toward those grisly, gleaming legs—

They vanished in the darkness. His plunging body encountered nothing but empty, evil-reeking space. He heard a slithering sound. . . . His eyes started from their sockets. The *legs* had appeared again—were glowing demonically in a far corner of the room!

Once more he sprang, hell-fury lending speed to his hurtling body. And as he leaped, he heard Doris Killian's sudden, choking scream from the bed. "Pat —*something's got me—!*" she shrieked. Her voice was cut off in a gurgling, retching moan of pure horror.

Dexter tried to halt himself in midair. And then his shoulder impacted against something soft, something that engulfed him in a black mantle. . . . His clutching hands closed about a soft, yielding shape that squirmed sinuously, weirdly. Arms—or were they tentacles? —wrapped themselves about him, holding him, binding him. . . .

He struggled, whipped his right fist free, smashed it forward with all the strength of his sinewy muscles. His knuckles sank deep into soft, yielding flesh. He struck again and again, savagely, insanely. The squirming form sagged against him, slipped to the floor.

Dexter whirled, oriented himself in the blackness, launched himself like a projectile in the direction of the bed. He pitched headlong across the covers as he misjudged the distance in the darkness. His body sprawled forward over twisting, struggling forms—

AS though in a nightmare, his hands encountered writhing, gripping fingers that were twisted viciously about Doris Killian's gasping throat. A sobbing curse rose to Dexter's lips.

He pried at those vise-like fingers, wrenched at them. Under him, a struggling body twisted around. A fist smashed into Dexter's mouth. He tasted the salt tingle of blood from his split lips. "Damn you to hell!" he snarled. His own knotted fists arced forward

In Next Month's

Spicy Mystery Stories

—

GODDESS of TERROR

By

WYATT BLASSINGAME

On Sale July 15th

through the dark, pounding into features that seemed queerly, weirdly muffled, blurred. . . .

With his antagonist, Dexter rolled off the bed, thumped to the floor. His head smashed against the woodwork; blinding lights cascaded before his staring eyes. For a single instant he was stunned.

And in that instant, he felt something hard, metallic, crashing again and again upon his skull. Blinded with pain, savage with rage, Dexter squirmed free, struggled to his feet. Instinctively his right hand shot forward, warding off another murderous blow.

His fingers closed about an iron-hard wrist. He twisted with all the magnificent strength of his muscular body; heard a sickening, snapping sound of broken bones. . . . A harsh voice rasped out a groan of tortured agony.

And as he heard that agonized cry. Dexter snarled in triumph. "You hell-fiend!" he bellowed. His balled fists rammed home against a sagging, semiconscious jaw, like twin pile-drivers. In the blackness, the unseen adversary slipped to the floor and lay in a motionless heap. . . .

Dexter shook his head to clear it. Then he sprang toward the wall, found the light-switch, clicked it. Nothing happened. "Turned off from the fuse-box outside!" Dexter rasped. He staggered toward the bureau, found his flashlight. Its blue-white circle of light sprang into life like a glaring eye. . . .

Doris Killian lay on the bed, wide-eyed, terror-palsied. Her throbbing throat was a mass of blue bruises; the nightgown had been ripped from her body, exposing her wildly heaving breasts. "Doris—are you all right?" Dexter cried out.

"Y-yes!" Her voice was a pathetic croak.

"Hold this light!" Dexter jammed the flashlight into her trembling fingers. Then, in the blue-white spray of illumination, he leaned over the form which he had beaten into unconsciousness. It was a man—clad in black from head to feet. A black hood shrouded his features; a black cloak engulfed him to the tips of coal-black shoes. Dexter ripped away the sinister hood-mask—

"God! *It's Tom Sloane—your brother-in-law!*" he whispered to Doris Killian.

The girl sobbed out a cry of unbelief. Her eyes widened as she looked down into the unconscious features of the grey-haired Tom Sloane, who had tried to murder her in the blackness of the room.

AND then Dexter had leaped across the room, to that other black-cloaked, black-hooded figure; the one he had smashed down before he had leaped to Doris Killian's rescue. He ripped the hood away. It was Edith Sloane—Tom Sloane's wife—Doris Killian's half-sister!

ABRUPTLY, Dexter reached forward and yanked the black cloak upward, away from the unconscious woman's legs. He stared. Edith Sloane's legs, her feet, her white thighs, were bare, naked. *And they were covered with luminous paint!* They were painted with grey, weirdly-glowing stuff, almost entirely to her naked loins!

"So that's how the trick was played!" Dexter whispered harshly. "She painted her nude legs with luminous paint. Then she stole into this room, in the darkness. Against the black background, her body and her face couldn't be seen. She held up the cloak, disclosing those weird legs—so that it appeared that the legs

were moving without a body! And when she lowered the folds of her cloak, the legs seemed to vanish in the darkness!"

"You—you mean that Edith—was the one who came here—earlier tonight—?" Doris Killian gasped faintly.

"Yes! She must have been! And she left those other legs—the amputated legs—in the room, along with the red-sealed envelope. Then, before I could recover my wits and spring out of bed, she got away. She went to my garage, let the air out of my tire. That gave her time to get home before I could follow her! Gave her time to steal the amputated legs out my room, while I was changing my tire!"

"But—but why? Why should Edith and Tom try to—murder me?" Doris moaned.

"I can see the whole thing now! Tom Sloane was administrator of the estate your father left you when he died. And he probably wanted the money himself—he and Edith would have inherited, had you died. And so they cooked up this scheme to kill you. And they tried to surround it with weird mystery—tried to throw the crime on Professor Astro, the fake mystic, whom they knew I had been hounding in my columns!"

"And—and the maid, Cecile?"

"Edith and Tom Sloane must have killed her. I don't know why—unless the maid overheard them plotting, and they had to do away with her to keep her mouth closed. Then they planted her legless body in Astro's house, to throw suspicion on Astro!" Dexter chuckled grimly, mirthlessly.

"No wonder Astro accused me of planting that corpse in his house! The poor devil was as startled as I was, when I discovered the dead body! I suppose he got loose while I was out phoning for the police—he ran away and took that damning corpse with him! Which would explain its disappearance!"

From the floor near the bed, there came a hollow groan. Tom Sloane stirred, tried to move his broken arm. His face turned grey-green in the weird light of the flashlight. "I—I heard what you've been—saying, Dexter. And you—guessed the truth. But it—was Edith's—plan from the—start. She made me—help her. And—I'll confess everything! I'll turn—State's evidence!"

EDITH SLOANE quivered, staggered to her feet, swayed. She started to run toward the door. Dexter caught her, held her in his vice-like arms. Defeated, thwarted, her eyes glared balefully. She spat venomously at her prone, helpless husband. "You spineless rat!" she hissed. That was all. But it was enough. It was her confession of guilt.

And then Dexter heard a thunderous pounding on his front door. Uniformed police burst into the house. They held Astro, the mystic, handcuffed in their midst. "We found the guy trying to sneak out of town, Mr. Dexter. And he had a naked, legless woman's corpse in his car!"

Dexter smiled. "Astro's innocent. He was a victim of circumstances. Here are your murderers. Take them away!" He pointed to Tom Sloane, and to Doris Killian's black-clad sister, Sloane's snarling wife.

Later, when they had all left, Dexter and the trembling, red-haired Doris Killian were once more alone together. Doris looked shyly into Pat Dexter's gentle eyes. "I—I guess I should go h-home, n-now," she faltered.

He pushed her tenderly back upon the bed. "You're already home, sweet. This is your home—from now on! You're staying here tonight; and every night,"

www.ingramcontent.com/pod-product-compliance
Lightning Source LLC
Chambersburg PA
CBHW051144020726
47501CB00005B/1670